WATER SKY

ALSO BY JEAN CRAIGHEAD GEORGE

The Cry of the Crow

Going to the Sun

The Grizzly Bear with the Golden Ears

Julie of the Wolves

The Moon of the Alligators

The Moon of the Bears

The Moon of the Chickarees

The Moon of the Deer

The Moon of the Fox Pups

The Moon of the Gray Wolves

The Moon of the Moles

The Moon of the Monarch Butterflies

The Moon of the Mountain Lions

The Moon of the Owls

The Moon of the Salamanders

The Moon of the Wild Pigs

The Moon of the Winter Bird

One Day in the Alpine Tundra

One Day in the Desert

One Day in the Prairie

One Day in the Tropical Rain Forest

One Day in the Woods

Shark Beneath the Reef

The Summer of the Falcon

The Talking Earth

The Wounded Wolf

Who Really Killed Cock Robin?
An Ecological Mystery

The Missing 'Gator of Gumbo Limbo
An Ecological Mystery

The Fire Bug Connection
An Ecological Mystery

WATER SKY

Jean Craighead George

HarperTrophy®
A Division of HarperCollins Publishers

Illustrations by the author

Thank you Patsy Aamodt, the David Brower family,

the bowhead whale research and census staffs

and the whalers of Barrow town

WATER SKY
Copyright © 1987 by Jean Craighead George
Printed in the United States of America.
All rights reserved.
Designed by Al Cetta

Library of Congress Cataloging-in-Publication Data
George, Jean Craighead, date
  Water sky.

  Summary: While searching for his uncle in Barrow,
Alaska, a young boy joins the crew of an Eskimo whaling
captain and learns the importance of whaling to the
Eskimo culture.

  1. Eskimos—Juvenile fiction. 2. Indians of North
America—Juvenile fiction. [1. Eskimos—Fiction.
2. Indians of North America—Fiction. 3. Whaling—
Fiction] I. Title.
PZ7.G2933Wat 1987   [Fic]   86-45496
ISBN 0-06-022198-4
ISBN 0-06-022199-2 (lib. bdg.)

  (A Harper Trophy book)
ISBN 0-06-440202-9

First Harper Trophy edition, 1989.

To

JOHN CRAIGHEAD GEORGE

Who made this book possible by taking me

With him out on the ice and introducing me

To the incredible bowhead whale and the

Sharing people of Barrow town

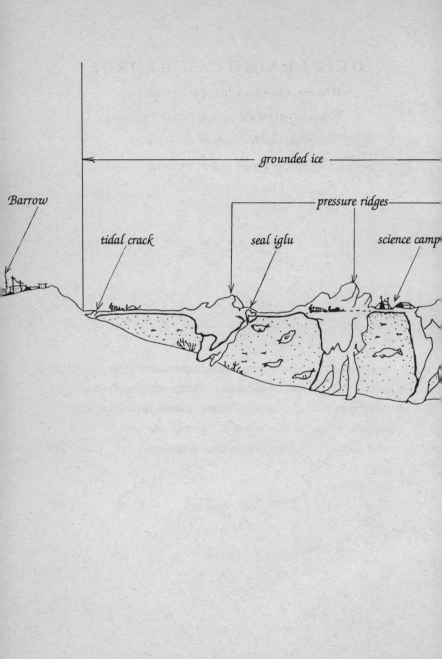

Barrow

grounded ice

pressure ridges

tidal crack

seal iglu

science camp

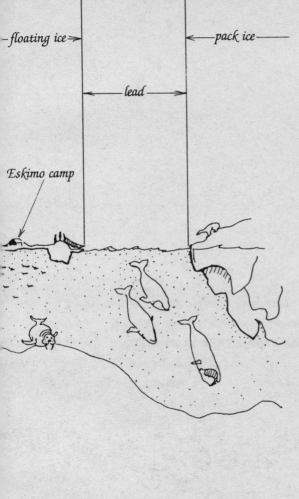

floating ice → ← pack ice

lead

Eskimo camp

Contents

WATER SKY

ONE

Lincoln

A BOY in a bright blue ski jacket and Maine hunting boots stood on a snowy runway. Under rumpled black hair his crooked nose and wide brown eyes gave him an expression of good humor, although he was not amused at this moment. Yesterday he had left Boston and laid over in Anchorage in high spirits. Now he was about to run back to the friendly jet that had carried him across Alaska to this barren Arctic outpost.

Suddenly, a cloud of frozen fog swirled over him. He could not see the plane, or the sky, or the flat snowscape that rolled endlessly out beyond the airport. Wrapped in an Arctic whiteout, he could have been upside down or sidewise for all he could tell. And so he stood still. In a few moments he was standing in the sunshine again, and the terror of the tundra blew off.

He turned and ran to the airport terminal, his face happy with purpose. He was going to do what he had come to Barrow, Alaska, to do. He did not look back again.

Inside the squat building he waited until his eyes adjusted to the dim light, then nervously scanned the faces of the people who had come to meet the passengers.

No face satisfied him. He repeated the words of the man to whom he and his father had talked by telephone several months ago.

"You will know me by my blue-rimmed sunglasses," Vincent Ologak had said. The boy glanced from face to face. There was no one with blue-rimmed sunglasses.

"You Lincoln Noah Stonewright?" The boy spun around, and his eyes met those of another boy.

"Yes, yes, I am."

"I am Kusiq." Kusiq wore a red woolen hat pulled down to his black eyebrows. A ruff of wolverine fur circled his darkly tanned face like a rising sun. He was dressed in white except for his sealskin boots. They were silver fur with a checkered border of black-and-white fur. As Lincoln shook Kusiq's hand, his family's old photographs of Eskimos came to mind. "I have walked into those pictures," he said to himself. "Everything is the same: the clothes, the boots, the faces." He stood quietly, wondering what to do next.

"How are you?" the young Eskimo asked. "I'm glad you're here." His exceptionally dark eyes were slanted upward as if he were perpetually smiling. His cheeks were broad and high, like those of the Eskimos in the painting that hung above the fireplace in Lincoln's home. It had been a centerpiece for his childhood thoughts on rainy days and snowy nights. The painting depicted his great-great-grandfather's whaling ship frozen into the

Arctic ice for the winter. Kids like Kusiq were playing baseball on the ice with the adult Eskimos and the Yankee whalers, as the whalers from Boston and New York were called. Lincoln managed to smile at Kusiq.

"Vincent Ologak is sorry he cannot meet you," Kusiq said. "He is not well."

Lincoln breathed deeply to quell the panic that was rising in him. For four months he had thought about this man who was going to meet him at the airport. When he awoke at night, he would clutch his pillow and wonder how living with an Eskimo family would go. Then he would think of Vincent Ologak, his father's good friend. "He was once mayor of the enormous North Slope Borough of eighty-eight thousand square miles and four thousand people," his father had said. "But he is soft-spoken. He is one of the best whaling captains who ever lived. But he loves all whales. He is a scientist who goes beyond technology. He knows what the animals think and what the sea ice says. But most important, he is a loving man—a big man." When Lincoln had thought about meeting Vincent Ologak, he had felt better about going so far from home and had gone back to sleep. Now he was frightened. Vincent Ologak was not here.

"Maybe," Lincoln said to himself, "Mom was right after all." She had not wanted him to take this trip to the Arctic. Alice Stonewright had never really said why, not even that it was dangerous or that she would miss him, but she had let his father know exactly how she felt.

"Frederick," she had said to Lincoln's father one April

evening shortly before Lincoln was to leave, "I'm going to say this once more. I don't think Lincoln should go to Barrow. It's not necessary—at all." Her sandy eyelashes had lowered over her pale-blue eyes too late to hide her anger.

"She's sure mad about this one," Lincoln had mused, then given up trying to understand what was going on between his mother and father. Fortunately they were all at dinner, seated at the big mahogany dining table in Lincoln's great-great-grandfather's house, which now belonged to his father. Lincoln could concentrate on balancing his peas on his knife instead of listening once more to this argument.

But there was no argument. His father did not answer. The only sounds Lincoln heard were the clicks of silverware against the china plates and the thumps of the waves hammering the bay shore at the bottom of the big lawn. The plans were firm.

Lincoln snapped back to the present, looked at Kusiq and swallowed hard.

"I'm sorry Vincent Ologak's sick," Lincoln managed to say, then quickly blurted, "I'll just go to the hotel. Dad said there's one here. I'll call him."

"Oh, you do not have to do that. I will take you to Vincent Ologak all right. He sent me to get you."

Lincoln managed to work his mouth into a smile. The wind struck the terminal with a mournful wolf howl. The building shuddered. He reached for his return ticket just as his baggage came through a large door in the metal-

[6]

walled building, together with a blast of cold air. Resolutely he picked up his duffel and suitcase.

"Okay," he said. "Please take me to Vincent Ologak."

"You cannot go as you are," Kusiq said. "You need Eskimo clothes. He is on the ice."

"I'll be all right," the boy said. "I've skied at zero in these clothes."

Kusiq smiled at him politely.

"I will take you home first. You can leave your bags there." Lincoln nodded. With his duffel in one hand, his suitcase in the other, he followed Kusiq out of the terminal.

At the top of the steps he looked out on the village of Barrow. It was not easy to see, for it was white on the white landscape. Everything was covered with hoarfrost—utility poles and wires, buildings, their doorways, and parked snowmobiles. The air glittered and flashed with what seemed to be smithereens of mica, but which was subzero mist. The cold was working its white magic to hide the little town at the top of the world.

"Hey, it's beautiful," Lincoln exclaimed. Then he saw two four-wheel-drive vehicles that had been left running so they would not freeze up while their drivers waited for their passengers. He also noticed that only one person walked the cold, white streets. And then he saw why. The large thermometer on the side of the terminal registered thirty-five below zero.

Lincoln's breath crystallized on his eyelashes, and he almost did not see Kusiq go around a mountain of plowed

snow. He ran down the steps and found him beside an orange snow machine. The sight of the big Ski-Doo not only cheered Lincoln but banished his doubts about staying in Barrow. From the looks of things he would be driving snow machines to get around, and that would be just great. His dad was right. This was going to be a wonderful adventure.

"Hop on," Kusiq said. "I'll give you a tour. Show you what finding oil on our ancestral land has done for the Eskimo."

Lincoln swung onto the seat behind Kusiq and balanced himself by holding a piece of luggage in each hand. The machine shot forward. He grabbed with his knees to keep from shooting backward into the snow.

Kusiq steered the machine around the snow pile and sped down the main street. The houses stood far back from the broad main drive. They were small to conserve heat. Some were almost buried under drifts of snow. When the sun hit them, they twinkled.

"I am not on my planet," Lincoln said to himself. "Barrow is not just 'different,' as Dad says; it is otherworldly."

Kusiq glanced back to make sure Lincoln was still on the snow machine and blew his warm breath into the wolverine fur on his parka hood. The fur held the warmth and made a tropical climate around his face. Kusiq was comfortably warm. Lincoln was not. In the short distance he had come, his face was aching with cold and his gloved hands were icy.

"High school," Kusiq shouted loud enough to be heard over the roaring motor. "The elders believe in education." Lincoln was impressed by the large and architecturally modern building.

"Got everything," Kusiq shouted. "Computers, video lab, shops, library, swimming pool, gym—cost seventy-three million." He beamed and swung the snow machine toward the center of town.

"Borough Hall." Kusiq pointed to an enormous wooden building that loomed above the little houses. It was marine blue in color and had strong lines and angles. Lincoln wondered how the builders had gotten all the materials that were in it to the Arctic. He knew supplies came by plane and boat, but they were small and the building was massive and three stories high.

"Stuaqpak!" Kusiq called as they passed a large red building. "Supermarket. First schools, then stores."

Lincoln was surprised to see that the stuaqpak was not unlike the supermarkets on the outskirts of New Bedford, Massachusetts, his hometown. He had hardly had time to think about this before they were crashing up and over snow piles and dodging around huge blocks of ice. Kusiq stopped the machine at the top of one of the largest piles.

"The Arctic Ocean," he said with a sweep of his arm. "Eskimos call it 'the ice.' "

Before them lay a frozen plain that became sky somewhere in the whiteness and cold.

"You are one thousand one hundred and fifty nautical miles from the North Pole." He cast Lincoln a wry glance and winked. "Good schools here all right," he said.

Lincoln squinted across the endless ice and snow.

"Vincent Ologak's out there," Kusiq said.

"Out there?"

"Yes. This is the whaling season, and Vincent Ologak is a whaling captain. He is not well. But he must help his people."

Kusiq looked hard at Lincoln. "You still want to go?"

"Yes." Lincoln's voice was barely audible, but he was resolute. "I still want to go."

Kusiq turned the snow machine around, bumped it down the ice hill and drove up to a small square house also white with hoarfrost.

"This is where I live," he said proudly of a plywood-and-tarpaper structure. The smoke that flowed out of its tin chimney looked glorious to Lincoln, for his toes and hands ached from the cold. Eagerly he followed Kusiq through the door.

They entered a small windowless room. Kusiq closed the front door, and they were immersed in darkness.

"This is the qanitchaq," Kusiq said. "Keeps the cold out of the iglu. Iglu is a house, by the way—all houses— not just a snow house." He opened a second door and preceded Lincoln into a wonderfully warm room, as cozy and as littered as a sparrow's nest. Lincoln dropped his bags and shook his hands to warm them.

His second impression was that he was at a garage sale. On the floor, tables and chairs were paper bags, boxes, furs, tools, skins and piles of clothing. Food sat out on tables as if ready to serve visitors. The stove top was jammed with pots, out of which stewed meaty bones protruded. Coffee percolated. Lincoln's third impression was that everything was for the taking. It did not have to be offered. It was being offered.

Finally, his fourth impression was that he was in a workshop. Bits of fur and hide were strewn around a sewing machine on which sat a half-finished boot. On a wooden crate lay carving tools, walrus tusks and whale bones. Pieces and parts of radios sat on the floor.

A CB receiver crackled. Lincoln was very surprised to see it. He studied it long enough to note that it was a very good make; then his eyes moved on. Against the wall three TVs were stacked one upon the other. Apparently only the top one worked, and it was turned on to a wrestling match. An elderly woman in a neat flowered dress sat in an overstuffed chair watching it. Her small, intent face was as wrinkled as the room was jumbled. The wrinkles curled upward, directing Lincoln's gaze to her intelligent eyes.

When a commercial came on, she turned to Lincoln.

"How are you? I am Annie. Sit down." She pushed a woolen sock and a sealskin boot off a chair. "You look like your father."

"She is speaking in English to you," Kusiq said. "That is very unusual for Annie. She never speaks in English to a tanik unless she likes him. Right Annie?"

She nodded.

"Tanik?" Lincoln asked.

"Our word for white person," Annie said.

"Annie's my great-grandmother," Kusiq went on. "She is a very important elder. She runs the school board. She is eighty-eight and remembers everything. She even remembers when the earth was upside down."

"It was upside down once?" Lincoln asked politely.

"Yes," Annie answered. "That was long ago, when the earth was just beginning and everything was dark. Then one day I saw the earth roll over and there was light."

"You remember that?" Lincoln asked incredulously, but with respect. Annie leaned forward.

"I wasn't really there. It just sounds more real if I say I saw how the world began."

A little girl crawled out of a pile of furs and blankets at the far end of the room. Since this was a one-room house, Lincoln concluded that the furs were the bedroom.

"How are you?" she said, walking up to Lincoln.

"Meet Loretta," said Kusiq. "She is one of Annie's adopted children. She has lots of adopted children."

"Annie," said Loretta, who had been listening to everything, "tell Lincoln Noah Stonewright how the people came."

"Please do," said Lincoln.

"It is said," began Annie, scrunching up her eyes, "it is said that when our sky was down under, there was a person, a wolf . . . wolves.

"While they were down there, a wolf had two children, a little girl and a little boy, and these two people multiplied and increased.

"It is said that from these wolves—this little girl and little boy—came all the people to multiply and increase.

"I call myself part wolf," she said. "To myself, of course." Her eyes twinkled like the hoarfrost.

"Now," said Loretta, "tell Lincoln Noah how the land came." She hugged Annie's knee.

"When the earth turned over, the boy was a man. The girl was a woman. All around them was water—a flood. The man saw an island. He threw his harpoon at the island and pulled it out of the sea. And so there was land."

"We have a story something like that," Lincoln said. "I mean about the flood."

Annie nodded.

"We know that story, too," said Loretta of the creamy-tan skin and black eyes. "It's about Noah, the man who loved animals. You have his name." She seemed very pleased with her knowledge, then added proudly, "We are Presbyterians."

"Same story all right," said Annie. "It came from us, the Iñupiat. Iñupiat means 'the real people.' We are the first people, and all the others are related to us, as the old stories show."

Annie made Lincoln feel very comfortable. With a few words and a lot of eye smiles, she had welcomed him into the sparrow's nest along with Loretta and Kusiq. He leaned back and relaxed for the first time since arriving in Barrow. He now knew he would accomplish what he had come to do. This trip to Barrow was more than "an adventure in growing up," as his father described it; Lincoln had come for his own reason—to find Jack James, his uncle.

Jack James, his mother's younger brother, had come to Barrow two years ago to stop the Eskimo from killing the rare and endangered bowhead whale. After sending Lincoln one postcard, he had written no more. Not even a phone call came from this brawny, yellow-haired man who was all men to Lincoln—father, brother, uncle and buddy.

When Lincoln had been only seven, Uncle Jack had rescued him from one of his mother's boring lawn parties. He had tweaked his sleeve; yelled, "Bet you can't catch me"; and run down the long sloping lawn to the beach,

Lincoln in pursuit. There they had found a killdeer's nest, a tidal pool and a broken oar. They had not returned until the party was over.

A few days later Uncle Jack had moved into Lincoln's house, a large Victorian mansion with a widow's walk on the roof and gingerbread on the porches. It stood on a knoll above the bay. Lincoln's great-great-grandfather, Amos Stonewright, had built the beautiful house for his wife, Nora, when he had returned from the Arctic with a fortune from whaling.

Uncle Jack fit into the household like a hermit crab in a seashell.

"Hey, sis," he would say to Lincoln's mother, "can I borrow your car? Linc and I want to go skiing." Or he would say, "Linc and I are going to spend a few days at the Gunks and go rock climbing."

Lincoln's parents liked the arrangement. Alice, his mother, was busy with tennis and volunteer work at the day-care center, as well as with the many parties she gave for friends and businesspeople. Having Jack entertain Lincoln was a good arrangement for her. Frederick, Lincoln's father, spent most of the week in Boston, where he worked in the family investment firm. Although he was gone much of the time, he and Lincoln did have a good time when they were together, especially when they went hunting in the Adirondacks. So Uncle Jack filled in lots of gaps.

Once he took Lincoln to a fox's den. They caught mice and watched the pups pounce on them. One summer

Lincoln and Jack spent almost the entire time sailing the old catboat along the Atlantic Coast. A violent storm struck them one day and carried them far out to sea. It took a great deal of ingenuity and energy to ride out the storm and get home.

The following summer Jack learned that the humpback whale migrated past Cape Cod, and he went to Woods Hole to study with a group of men and women who were tracking the whales. He came back for Lincoln, and together they sailed around the Cape recording the activities of a mother and her baby.

"Mankind has no right," said Jack on that trip, "to push the whales to extinction." Lincoln agreed. He agreed with anything Uncle Jack said.

The next April Uncle Jack picked up Lincoln at his school one afternoon and drove him home. They sat side by side on the warm granite steps that looked over the bay.

"Linc," Jack had said, "I'm going to the Arctic. I'm going to see your father's friend, Vincent Ologak. I must educate him. The Eskimo must stop whaling." Uncle Jack rubbed his hands over his smooth, sun-burned chin.

"You're going to the Arctic?" Lincoln was devastated. "Will you take me?"

"Can't do it. But I won't be there long." Lincoln sat very still to keep back the tears. Then Uncle Jack hugged him.

"I'll write," he said, slapped him across the back and was gone.

One postcard arrived. Lincoln wrote back a five-page letter, but it never reached its destination. It was returned "address unknown." Lincoln waited a month, the month became a year, then eighteen months and still no word from Uncle Jack. When he asked his mother why Uncle Jack never wrote to him, she shrugged her shoulders. "I hate to write letters too," she replied.

Lincoln was hurt and concerned. Something was not right, but he did not know what or what to do about it.

Fortunately, several days before Christmas, Lincoln's father asked him to join him in the library.

"When I was your age, Lincoln," he began, "I spent a spring and summer in Barrow, Alaska, where your great-great-grandfather, Amos Stonewright, whaled.

"I lived with the Vincent Ologak family. It was an unforgettable experience. I'd like you to have such an experience too. I'm making arrangements for you to stay with my old friend just as I did." His father's dark eyes grew mellow, and he ran his fingers through his thick black hair.

"Your mom's against this. . . ." He did not finish.

That was more than four months ago. Now here he was in this crowded little house about to meet Vincent Ologak and find Uncle Jack. He watched Kusiq toss clothes from a box like a fox scattering earth.

"Your parkie is somewhere here," Kusiq said. "I'll find it. Loretta, look through the clothes on the couch."

Annie finally turned off the TV and got up to help. She was slight of figure and quite bent at the shoulders, but her steps were quick and sure. She sorted the scattered clothing.

"Annie knows how to do everything," Kusiq said as he gave up the search. "She can make clothes, make skin boats, fish, hunt. She can do everything necessary to life; also dance and sing. She grew up in a sod house. Do you know what a sod house is?"

Lincoln shook his head.

"That," he said, pointing to a photograph on the wall, "is a sod house."

A mound of earth was pictured. In front of it stood a small woman. She was touching a tunnel of sod bricks propped up by the huge rib bones of a whale. The tunnel went downward, then up, locking out the wind and cold from the sod house like the qanitchaq. The woman was a younger Annie, but she had the same bright eyes, delicate nose and high cheeks.

"She lived there until her husband died," Kusiq said. "She cooked on a stone—a whale-oil stove—softened hides with her teeth, sewed them, raised nine babies to be men and women. She heated the house with whale blubber, made baskets from whale baleen and tools from whale bones."

Lincoln was interested in all the uses the Eskimo had for whales. Had Uncle Jack been told this? If so, had it changed his mind about Eskimo whaling? What had happened to him?

"The whale," Kusiq said quietly, "is our hardware store. We use aġviQ—Iñupiat for bowhead whale—for houses, sleds, traps, fishlines, bows, art and even brooms."

"But not anymore," Lincoln said, repeating Uncle Jack's favorite line as he gestured to cardboard boxes and plastic chairs. "You have other materials. You don't need to kill whales anymore."

There was a long silence. A long silence. He had said something wrong—very wrong. He looked to Annie for help. She was gazing quietly at Kusiq, whose face was crisscrossed with lines of anger. Annie did not take her eyes from him until the lines had disappeared and Kusiq's face reflected patience. Lincoln had the eerie feeling that the two had been talking without words, then shrugged off the thought.

Annie leaned over a cardboard box.

"Here's your parkie," she said, holding up an ingeniously tailored coat of sheepskin, wool side in. Annie had bought the skin at the stuaqpak and trimmed it with rare and frost-resistant wolverine.

Lincoln re-dressed without protest. He put on wool underwear, pants, socks, shirt. Over his shirt went a down vest, over his pants down overalls. He pulled on the parka and was grateful to be looking through a circle of wolverine fur. He blew into it, felt the warmth inside and was relieved to find that Kusiq's trick worked. Finally Annie handed him a white snow shirt, a loose nylon parka to put over his skin parka.

"Whaling crews wear white," Kusiq said. "The whales perceive people in dark clothes and swim away."

"But," said Lincoln, "I'm not going whaling. I just

want to talk briefly to Vincent Ologak." He had seen that wind-carved sea of ice. "I'm—I'm supposed to go to school while I'm here. I'll just go out to whale camp and come right back after I talk to Vincent Ologak."

"It may take you a long time to talk to Vincent Ologak," Kusiq said. "He is very busy. He is whaling."

Lincoln did not understand how this could be, but when Kusiq handed him fur-lined gloves and fur-lined mittens to pull over them, he shrugged and put them on.

Annie came out of the qanitchaq with a regal pair of knee-high boots. They were made of sealskin, and around the top of each was a white band of fur into which black sleds and sled dogs were sewn. Lincoln gasped to see such beautiful boots.

"Ugruligs," she said, "knee boots. I made them for you of ringed seal fur and the hide of the bearded seal, our friends of the ocean."

"For me? You made them for me?" Lincoln felt truly welcomed and held them in his hands staring at them for a long time. When Annie gave him a pair of felt boots to make them warmer, he put them on and slid his feet into the ugruligs. Up from his feet, into his knees, his thighs, his stomach and brain, surged the warmth. His feet were not going to freeze off, as he had fully expected them to do, if the ride from the airport was a sample of travel in the Arctic.

Kusiq flipped a walrus-hide rope over Lincoln's head and tied it around his waist.

"So the wind will not blow up your shirt and freeze

you," he said. Lincoln accepted. The snowmobile ride had taught him respect for the wind.

Annie stepped back and contemplated him.

"You look like an Eskimo all right. No one will hurt you."

"Hurt me?"

"Eskimos do not like white men on the ice when they are whaling," Kusiq said.

Lincoln was startled. "I don't want to go out on the ice if I'm not wanted. I can speak to Vincent Ologak when he comes in."

"He may never come in. He is very ill," Annie replied. "No one will hurt you. You will be all right. You are a relative."

"A relative?"

"Your great-great-grandfather married Vincent's and my husband's aunt, Nora Ologak."

Lincoln stood stock-still.

"Wow!" he said. "Wow!"

Thoughtfully he looked from Annie to Kusiq to Loretta.

"I didn't know that," he said, then added, "That's neat." He pushed back the wolverine ruff and rubbed the almost-invisible fuzz on his chin.

"I wonder why no one ever told me great-great-grandma Nora was an Eskimo."

No one answered him.

Kusiq opened a wooden closet and rummaged through it. After a moment he drew out a rifle and passed it to Lincoln.

"For me?"

"For polar bears," said Kusiq. "They attack us out on the ice. Very dangerous animals. They do not fear people."

Lincoln turned the gun over in his hands, cranked open the bolt, found the chamber empty and took a sighting on a paper bag in a corner.

"Your father was a good shot," Annie said. "He could hit a caribou a quarter mile away." She patted Lincoln's arm to say he could, too.

Kusiq gave Lincoln a handful of cartridges, which, as his father had taught him to do, he put into his pocket, not into the gun.

"No, not there," Kusiq said. "Keep your gun loaded always. Bears are very fast." He picked out a rifle for himself and escorted Lincoln to the door.

"Now we see Vincent Ologak," he said.

TWO

Aullaagvik, the whale camp

LINCOLN tested his new boots by digging them into the snow while Kusiq bolted a long wooden sled to the orange snow machine. Onto the sled he loaded batteries, cans of coffee, a crate of seamen's pilot biscuits, kerosene and a crate of peanut butter.

"Supplies for the whalers," Kusiq said, covering them with caribou skins, then lashing the skins down to tie loops on the side of the sled with a nylon rope. He blew on his bare hands and turned to Lincoln.

"Ride the sled," he said. "This one likes to go sidewise all right."

Without telling Lincoln where to stand and how to ride the sled, Kusiq pulled the starter cord. Fortunately, Lincoln had seen enough wilderness movies to grab a rail on the sled's backboard and step up on what was obviously a foot board. He waited to be corrected if he was wrong or praised if he was right. Kusiq did not even look back. With a jerk that wrenched Lincoln's shoulders and nearly dumped him into the snow, Kusiq started out along a trail carved into the ice by the whalers' snow machines.

Ten minutes later he stopped the machine and walked back to Lincoln.

"Hudson Bay start." He smiled. "White man taught us that. You always forget something when you start an expedition. So you go a little way and stop. The Hudson Bay furriers paddled half a day, then made camp. If they forgot something, they weren't far from the trading post.

"Good trick. I go ten minutes and stop." He took out a list and checked it, then looked at Lincoln.

"You need a face mask. Your face will freeze and peel. The thermometer at the airport said it was thirty-five below. It will be fifty or sixty below in the wind on the sled. Also wear your dark glasses, or you'll get snow blindness." He turned the machine around and drove wildly back to his house for the mask. Lincoln went to his duffel for his glasses and put them on.

They shot off again. On Kusiq's second start the steel cleats on the snowmobile cut so rapidly into the ice, they created a small blizzard. The machine leaped forward and they zoomed along, leaving a trail of snow like the vapor trail behind a jet.

In a short time Kusiq snarled the machine up a mountain of ice boulders with the shine and color of huge shattered Coke bottles. Here the trail had been laboriously hand cut in the blasting cold by the whalers. At the top Lincoln looked down on a different scene.

"End of the land-fast ice," Kusiq yelled over the roar of the machine. "Beginning of the floating ice—pan ice." Lincoln got off the sled and walked forward.

"Land-fast ice," Kusiq explained, "is ice that is grounded on the bottom of the ocean. Pretty safe. Where the sea-floor drops off, the ice floats. Pretty dangerous." He gave a gleeful whoop and yanked the starter cord. Lincoln barely had time to get back to his post before they were crashing down the glassy mountain onto the floating pan. As they sped along smoothly, Lincoln watched Kusiq so he could learn how to drive a snow machine. While he made mental notes, the sled swung far to the right. He was figuring out how to get it back on course when it jerked and shot far to the left.

No instructions came from Kusiq, but Lincoln was a skier. The next time the sled lurched to the left, he threw his weight to the right. The sled came into line behind the machine, but he overcompensated, and it shot off to the right. Lincoln threw his weight to the left and brought it back to center.

In this exhilarating manner, bending his knees and swinging, Lincoln kept the sled tracking as they flew over the pan ice, which was sky blue in color and pocked with craters like the moon.

Fortunately, he knew nothing of the dangers of the floating ice. To him it was solid and beautiful. He looked around with pleasure as the machine growled over flats and zipped past ice blocks that seemed to be lit from inside with cold turquoise lights. He did not know that he was riding over 150 feet of cold seawater on ice that was sometimes only two or three feet thick, nor did he know that the pan ice could move and pile itself up into mountains, or break off and float out toward Siberia.

The snow machine crashed on into whiteness, and Lincoln kept steering the recalcitrant sled. In the excitement of mastering it without being instructed, he forgot the fright he had suffered when Vincent Ologak had failed to meet him. He was having a wonderful time. He swung his body right and left, dipped his knees and rode the terrible wooden bronco with glee. When Kusiq finally looked back to see if he was still there, Lincoln waved and steered with his knees and one hand. He was in tune with the sled and the wilderness.

In crystalline air they banged up a ridge and down it, and shot across a plate of flat ice. A flock of king eider ducks flew by, quacking to keep in touch with each other as they migrated like a swarm of bees to their summer nesting grounds along the Arctic rivers. Lincoln whooped to the birds.

Turning into the sun, Kusiq drove the machine and sled to the top of a steep ice hill, where the Ski-Doo shuddered and almost stopped. He gave it gas. It took off, sailed through the air and landed on the pan with a splintering crash. The machine and sled held together. Lincoln cheered once for the flight, once for the landing— and once for his clothing. Kusiq stood up, twisted his body and grinned from ear to ear.

Although Lincoln could feel the bite of the cold on his

forehead, he was gloriously warm thanks to Annie. Not even the ice crystals that were sailing past like arrows penetrated his mask. He was thoroughly enjoying himself. They roared on.

After a while Lincoln wondered what time it was. His plane had landed at nine P.M. in broad daylight and it was still broad daylight. He could not guess and did not care. Riding a sled must be the wonderful experience his father wanted him to have.

Presently Kusiq snarled the machine up a ridge, turned off the engine and walked back to Lincoln. He pointed to a charcoal-gray cloud that hung between white ice and white sky.

"Water sky," he said. "Good cloud. It tells the Eskimo where the leads are. Leads are open water. They are rivers in the sea ice. Leads open and close. They are very dangerous. Only brave men camp near them. Very brave men. You'll be camping near a lead."

"Who, me?" He stared at the ominous cloud and added weakly, "I really ought to go to school tomorrow."

Kusiq flicked an eyebrow. "Up the leads," he said as though he had not heard, "come the great, huge, beautiful bowhead whales." His arms rose and fell as he mimicked their swimming motions.

"Up the leads come the aġviQs diving and breathing, diving and breathing.

"Up the leads they come, migrating from the Bering Sea, where they spend the winter, to the eastern Beaufort, where they spend the summer." Kusiq seemed to be almost singing. His voice rose and fell, his knees bent and his feet trod out a rhythm.

"They come alone, in twos, eights, in families, by the thousands." He paused. "They dive, surface and breathe; dive, surface and breathe.

"They come near the villages. The Eskimo whalers go out on the ice. They sing to them. And the whales come in on their songs.

"When a whale is taken," Kusiq concluded, "all fighting ceases among the Eskimo.

"We do not get mad at our brothers and sisters. Mothers and fathers stop arguing and hug each other. Neighbors hug. We do not hate the white men. Whaling time is beautiful. You'll be with us. You'll see."

"I must call my parents."

Kusiq heard. He took off his wool cap and ran his fingers through his straight black hair that was plastered in sweaty swaths to his wide forehead, and his mouth dropped open at the remark. Lincoln stared at the endless sea ice. It stretched on forever before and behind him, to his right and his left. It was even coming down as crystals from the sky. He eyed Kusiq and chuckled. Kusiq chuckled. Lincoln laughed. Kusiq laughed. They bent over in a fit of glee, clutching at their bellies. Finally Kusiq recovered and stood up.

"You Eskimo now," he said.

After another long run they pulled up beside a ship-shaped iceberg that jutted forty feet above the flat sea ice. Kusiq squinted at it.

"Icebergs," he said, "wander around our summer ocean like lost seal pups. Some stay too long and get stuck for the winter, like this one." Lincoln scrambled closer to it.

"That must be what happened to my great-great-grandfather's ship."

"Oh, yes, that is what happened to the Yankee whaling ships all right. Most got scrunched to bits. Ships do not know how to live here. Icebergs do. We name them puktaaq." Kusiq patted the monster named puktaaq as if it were a pet.

"We are almost to Vincent Ologak," Kusiq said. "Aullaagvik, the whale camp, is on the other side of the iceberg. We stop here briefly.

"The mound of white ice at our feet is pure ice, old, old ice—piqaluyk. The salt has leached out of it. We chip off chunks and melt them for drinking water."

"How did the clean ice get here?"

"Ivuqpagman ivuvlugu inuillu payagniu-lammata."

"What does that mean?"

"Silam, nature-m." Lincoln thought he must be saying that nature had brought the good ice to the Eskimos. But he wondered why Kusiq was suddenly speaking in Iñupiat, his native language. Was he trying to tell him that the whalers, like Annie, would speak to him in English only if they liked him?

Perhaps he would not be able to ask Vincent Ologak where Uncle Jack was, after all.

The wind blew. Ice crystals struck Lincoln's glasses. The cold grabbed like a vise. He felt far away from civilization. Although Kusiq had mentioned they would go only four miles from Barrow by measure, by time he felt as if he were a thousand years away. He took a long, deep breath and thought of Uncle Jack.

Kusiq stretched out a tarp and swung his axe, and huge chips of piqaluyk shattered and fell on the trail. Lincoln saw what was to be done and tossed the chips onto the tarp. He worked quickly. It was now quite evident that he was not going to be told what to do by these people. He would have to observe and figure things out for himself. He found he did not mind this at all. It made him feel grown up.

The piqaluyk loaded, Kusiq started off again. He sped the rig around the iceberg and came to a halt in a snow machine parking lot, a circle of mechanical beasts in the primeval icescape.

"From here we walk," said Kusiq, unhitching the sled. "We are quiet in whale camp . . . no machines."

He took hold of the shaft, Lincoln grabbed it too, and in silence they walked into whale camp, aullaagvik.

Whale camp was a large wall tent covered with a white parachute for insulation. It was set up about a hundred feet from the marine-blue water that was indeed a river, as Kusiq had said. Its banks were ice.

On the ice bank sat a beautiful umiaq, the Eskimo whaling boat of willow frame covered with bearded-sealskins. The stern was propped up so that the bow pointed into the water, ready to go. The umiaq glowed like a lamp as the setting sun shone through its paper-thin cover. Paddles stood upright for swift snatching. "What a beauty," Lincoln said.

Not far from the umiaq a man stood on a mound of ice at the water's edge. Some distance away stood another lonely figure. Both were facing the sea, watching for whales. They did not move—at all.

Lincoln looked around, expecting to see more things in whale camp, but there was nothing more. One tent, one boat, and four sleds was it.

And then he sensed one more thing—silence. It was as real as the tent. He stepped closer to Kusiq.

"Do whales hear?" he whispered.

He nodded.

"Underwater?"

He nodded again.

"They can also smell. Pee on land side of the tent."

Lincoln saw that there was no outhouse. He hoped he would be back at Annie's house before morning.

Kusiq and Lincoln pulled the sled to the front of the tent. A frozen seal and two eider ducks lay near the door. "Dinner," Lincoln said to himself, and was glad Kusiq had brought out the peanut butter.

The wind whistled up and down its own musical scale with eerie monotony. The ice creaked and moaned. The men on watch stood still—and waited. No painting or photograph, no words from his father, had prepared Lincoln Noah Stonewright for this.

Kusiq touched his arm.

"Vincent Ologak is waiting for you."

THREE

Vincent Ologak

VINCENT OLOGAK sat with his legs out straight
in a nest of golden caribou skins. He was in shirt sleeves
playing pinochle with a short husky man and a lean teen-
ager.

The whaling captain's back was harpoon straight. He
held his head high, like the leader of a wolf pack or the
president of a people. The men who were playing cards
with him were slightly bowed in unconscious respect.

The whaling captain glanced at Lincoln, nodded and
went back to the game, playing each card with slow grace,
as if he had never heard of time.

Vincent Ologak was a man of moderate size. He wore
a mustache and a neat tufted beard on his chin. His thick
black eyebrows arched to meet a cap of white hair cut
square across his forehead. He had the most peaceful face
Lincoln had ever seen.

While Lincoln waited, he noted that the tent was hushed
except for the hiss of water simmering in a huge kettle

on a kerosene heater. The steam and heater had warmed the air, and Lincoln untied his hood and let the ruff flop back. It circled his shoulders with a wreath of mahogany-colored fur, and he hoped he looked as elegant as Kusiq did when he dropped his hood back.

On the floor of the tent to his left sat a two-burner Coleman camp stove on which a large pot of soup simmered and coffee percolated. A woman with skin the color of a doe's, with short, neat hair squatted in front of the stove. She lifted a frying pan from a large wooden box that held food and kitchen utensils and, after putting it down, smiled at Lincoln. Her face was so friendly that he felt as if he had met her before, although he had not. She must be Bertha, Vincent's wife, he decided, because the wives of whaling captains, his father had told him, were the managers—planners, shoppers, hostesses and gift givers. They were also skin-boat stitchers, and a rare few were whale-camp cooks.

"How are you?" she said, concentrating on the heavy pan.

"Real good, thank you. I had a great flight into whale camp with Kusiq on the snow machine." Lincoln smiled broadly. Bertha went on with her work.

Behind the pleasant woman the tent space was piled with furry hides and down bags. Lincoln thought there were at least three men wrapped up and sleeping there.

In front of the sleeping area was a CB radio, on top of which sat a digital clock. It read eleven P.M., yet the sun was still above the horizon and illuminating the tent well enough to read by. Beginning on May 10th precisely—and it was now approaching the second of May—the sun would not set again for two and a half months, pouring light on the Arctic all day and all night. Sunshine attends the whale hunters.

The pinochle game ended. Vincent coughed and bent over as if in pain. Laboriously he straightened up and beckoned to Lincoln.

"Sit down, Lincoln Noah Stonewright."

Lincoln was startled by Vincent Ologak's voice. It sounded more like low-toned bells pealing in the distance than a man speaking. It was a very comforting voice, and Lincoln relaxed and took off his parka, although no one had invited him to. Bertha stuffed it, along with everyone else's, beside the cold tent walls for added insulation.

Crossing his legs, Lincoln sat down on a skin. His eyes leveled with the elder's. Again he was surprised. He had expected to see the keen eyes of a man who was a hunter, a whaling captain, a politician—eyes that were sharpened by cunning bouts with raw nature as well as with raw men. What he saw were the steady eyes of a serene human being.

"I'm glad you're here," Vincent Ologak said.

"Well, I'm really glad to see you," Lincoln replied sincerely. "My dad admires you so much." That did not seem to flatter the man, so he went on: "He told me how you killed a polar bear with a knife." The whaling captain's face did not change; everyday stuff, it said. Lincoln tried again.

"He also told me how you rescued him from a chunk

of ice that had broken off and was floating away." At last Vincent Ologak reacted. He stroked his beard and grinned.

"Your father I named 'the crazy one.' He was a little reckless all right." He smiled and shook his head. "But he was a good boy. He learned fast."

Lincoln had never thought of his father ever being a boy, much less being crazy and reckless. He grinned and felt better about his crooked nose. He had broken it when he had fallen from a lamppost he had foolishly climbed to show off for the love-of-his-third-grade-life.

"I've wanted to meet you for a long time," Lincoln said. "I've heard so much about you from Dad. But I also have another reason." Lincoln flashed the engaging Stonewright smile that had gotten the men of the family both into and out of trouble many times.

"My Uncle Jack, Jack James, came to Barrow two years ago. After a short time he stopped writing. We have not heard from him since." Vincent Ologak's expression did not change.

"Do you know what became of him?"

Sagniq, the older pinochle player, curtly introduced himself and his son, Tigluk, then left the tent. Tigluk put on his parka with loud remarks in Iñupiat and movements so exaggerated that Lincoln was forced to duck his head. When the father and noisy son had departed, Lincoln went on.

"The day before Uncle Jack left home, he told me he was going to meet you. If you don't know where he is, could you tell me how to go about finding him?"

Tigluk came back and picked up his rifle. As he brushed

past Lincoln, he jabbed him in the kidneys with the toe of his boot. The pain was so fierce, Lincoln bit his lips to keep from yelling. Vincent, who had bent over to cough, did not see the lightning-fast kick.

But Bertha sensed that something was wrong. She peeked through the tent flap at the retreating Tigluk, then looked quizzically at Lincoln. He smiled.

"I'll bet you're hungry all right?" she said. "Would you like hot soup?" He was so happy that Vincent and Bertha Ologak had been speaking to him in English that he quickly forgot Tigluk.

"Soup sounds real good, Mrs. Ologak. Yes, thank you."

Bertha ladled out a bowl of soup from the black pot and passed it to Lincoln, together with a big round pilot cracker. After a brief wait for a spoon he concluded there would be none. He brought the bowl to his mouth and sipped the brew. The beak of a duck floated to the surface. He stopped drinking.

"Perhaps you prefer peanut butter," Vincent Ologak said, interpreting the pause.

"No, no. This is good."

Lincoln took a big swallow. The beak rolled to the bottom, and several feathers surfaced. His stomach churned. He wondered what to do. He could not throw up. That would be an insult to his host and hostess. He could not pitch the soup out. Food must be scarce out here. He recalled a family story about Uncle Jack. At an important dinner party he had found a fly in his soup. Rather than embarrass his hostess, he had closed his eyes and swallowed it.

Lincoln closed his eyes and swallowed. Unseen, the brew was quite tasty. He was also very, very hungry, which helped.

When he opened his eyes, Vincent Ologak was looking at him with great fondness.

But he did not tell him where Uncle Jack was, or even if he knew how to go about finding him.

Lincoln was beginning to understand he would have to bide his time with these people of nature. They paced themselves slowly.

When he was done, he wiped his cup with a paper towel Bertha had given him and put it back in the box against the cold tent wall. What moisture was left on it was ice in seconds. Food preservation was no problem here. Everything near the tent walls was frozen, even the pilot biscuit. It had snapped like an icicle when he had bitten into it.

The furs in the sleeping area rustled, and a robust man yawned and got to his feet, completely dressed. Apparently he had slept with his clothes on. Bertha gave him a cup of coffee and a bowl of duck soup. He nodded to Lincoln as if he already knew all about him, then put on his parka and sunglasses. He picked up his gun and walked into the whiteness.

"That is Utik," Vincent said. "He's president of the bank. He's going on watch. We take turns sleeping and eating and watching for whales." He handed Lincoln a pair of binoculars.

"You go with him. You will learn from him. We need your eyes. I do not stand watch anymore." He coughed until his body crumpled over. With great concern Bertha put her arm around him and offered him a steaming bowl of duck soup. He smiled lovingly at her and shook his head.

"I cannot eat."

Bertha's lower lip trembled.

"You must," she said coaxingly; then her face brightened. "Lincoln Noah got the luscious beak; but I saved the best for you—the eyes."

Lincoln put on his parka, snow shirt and two gloves and two mittens, which took him a good ten minutes, picked up his gun and stepped out into the frigid twilight.

He caught up with Utik near the umiaq perch. Respecting the rule of silence, he gestured, "Will you show me what to do?" but did not think he had gotten his message across.

"We can talk out loud," Utik replied. "The whales have stopped coming." He sniffed the frosty air as if to smell their whereabouts.

"They come in three waves or runs. Thousands swim by for days and days, then none at all for days and days. Now we have none. The first run is over." He picked up a handful of snow and tossed it into the air.

"Eskimo weather vane," he said. "The wind is from the northeast. That is good. The northeast wind blows the pack ice away and opens the leads. Up the leads comes agvik.

"He follows the ice. He is an Eskimo all right, like the polar bear and seal; like the walrus and eider duck. We all stay close to the edge of the ice."

"What does the bowhead whale eat, sir?"

"Brit and krill, which are tiny, tiny lobsters and shrimp and crabs and snails and fragments of sea urchins—the plankton mass."

"The same as the humpback whale," Lincoln remarked.

Utik did not take his eyes off the darkening water. "A big whale needs two tons of brit and krill a day."

"Two tons of food a day!" Lincoln exclaimed. Even the scientists at Woods Hole had not told him this. "Wow. How can they eat that much?"

"With big mouths. I've seen bowheads with twenty-foot-long mouths. Inside are tiers and tiers of baleen—some people call them filters. AġviQ opens his mouth, the seawater runs in, he closes his mouth and shoots the water out through the filters with his tongue. The brit and krill are caught. He swallows."

"Baleen is what my great-great-grandfather made his fortune on."

"Yes, he and others." Utik shook his head. "They took a lot. One season the sea was red with the blood of thousands of bowheads—just for the baleen. The whalers did not render the oil, eat the meat or use the bones. They just slaughtered, took the baleen and left the rest to rot." He rubbed his chin. "Sacrilege." Lincoln pulled uneasily on his mittens and wondered why he, the great-great-grandson of a Yankee whaler, had been brought to whale camp.

"Then the Yankee whalers left the Arctic," Utik said.

"Because there were no more whales?"

"Essentially; after the great slaughter it was not worth their time to hunt. Also, petroleum products and spring steel replaced whale oil and baleen."

"They killed a lot?"

"Eighteen thousand in fifty years." Utik adjusted his parka hood. "But there were some left. They came every spring, increasing little by little. The Eskimo took about ten or twenty a year; but most often none. There were only a few crews then. Most Eskimos had forgotten how to whale.

"The whales came and went, and they increased. Then in the 1970s the taniks decided that the bowhead was going extinct.

"They called an international meeting. They ordered us to stop killing whales. The taniks came to the Arctic to tell us to eat chicken and hamburgers. We did not like those white knights."

Lincoln felt a chill go up his spine. Uncle Jack was one of them.

"We got mad all right. We, of all people, do not want to push the whale off the earth. The whale and the Eskimo are one.

"And we got mad because we were told not to hunt whales by the very people who had slaughtered them.

"And we got mad because the taniks do not think we know anything about whales. We know there are not as many as there were, but we also know there are enough to keep us whaling. We don't take many. We don't need many. We take only what we need.

"When the order to stop whaling went out, we got our own committee of Eskimos together and talked to the international crowd. They listened to our needs and decided on a compromise—the quota system we have now. This year Barrow can take four whales, Wainwright two, and the other seven whaling towns one to three according to the number of people living there.

"The quotas should be higher," Utik declared. "There are many more whales than the white men say. But we are good Americans. We are law-abiding. When we get our quota, we stop whaling."

Lincoln wondered why he was tolerated in whale camp at all—his Eskimo blood that had made him acceptable was very thin. Yet, curiously, he sensed he was wanted.

Utik stopped walking, took two sticks from his parka pocket, and bent over a four-inch-wide and very long crack in the ice. He placed one stick on one side of the crack and the second on the other side so that their points touched.

He walked along the crack for about forty paces and placed two more in the same way.

Gesturing to Lincoln to follow, he stepped out on powder-blue ice and walked to the umiaq perch.

"This is new ice," he said. "Forms along the edges of the leads when the water is still. Only a few inches thick." As he walked he put his whole foot down, not the heel then the toes as comes naturally. Lincoln wondered why until, walking naturally, he saw the spongy new ice sag and splinter, starlike, under his boot. He put his whole foot down and followed Utik in the stride the Eskimo learned from the polar bear, who walks the ice.

Utik climbed up to Ernie, who was standing watch on the umiaq perch, and tapped his arm, and Ernie departed. Utik signaled Lincoln to come up and take his place. The bank president then tipped back his head and blew skyward, making a breath geyser in the frigid air that looked like a whale blow. Lincoln understood that he should not talk anymore, and that he should stand stone still and watch for whales.

Utik walked to the other perch and relieved Waldo, "the smiler," a nickname Lincoln would soon learn was very appropriate. The genial man worked for *The Tundra Times*, "Farthest North Newspaper in the World"—he was in charge of the typing and layouts.

Lincoln looked over at Utik to learn what to do. Utik placed his feet close together to conserve warmth. Lincoln put his feet close together. Utik stuck his hands up his sleeves to make himself more compact. Lincoln stuck his hands up his sleeves and felt warmer. Utik turned his head slowly from right to left like an owl scanning a field for mice. And Lincoln turned his head slowly from right to left as he took up the vigil of whale watcher.

After a short time his mind began to wander. It wandered from Vincent to Annie to his mother and father and finally to Uncle Jack. What had happened to him? Was he hated? Was he even alive?

Lincoln suddenly felt weary from his toes to the top of his head. This had been a long, long day.

Fighting sleep, he watched the whaleless waters. A seal popped its head up and looked at him with black watery eyes. Lincoln whistled, and the animal came so near he could see its long, curved whiskers. The seal chirped and dove out of sight.

From the tent came the sound of singing.

"Nukik, Nukik, whale of Barrow," the whalers began in Iñupiat.

"Come to us, come to us. Great whale, hear us sing.

"Our ice cellars, which are dug deep into the tundra, have been cleaned to please you.

"The pots shine. The floors of our houses are swept.

"Come to us, Nukik. Come to us."

The melody rose and fell like waves hitting a beach. It throbbed like bears walking. It reached notes as high as the screams of the sea-ice winds. The men seemed to be out in the open. He stole a quick look. Three whalers, including Waldo, who wore a red snow-shirt belt, were on their knees singing to the whale of Barrow, calling to him. Lincoln was deeply stirred by the intensity of their faces and their haunting music, even though he could not understand the words.

The sun went below the horizon. Shortly it was day again. The sun was up. The sea ice sparkled. The mist that hung over the open water turned pink.

Lincoln's eyes grew heavy. He stared at the pack ice, trying to keep awake, and then, when he thought he could fight sleep no longer, Sagniq, the burly pinochle player, tapped his arm. Gratefully Lincoln slid down the perch and stumbled into the tent. He dropped into the skins without even taking off his parka and was instantly asleep.

The whalers sang through the night that was day and into the day that was always morning. Lincoln did not hear them. He slept like a hibernating grizzly bear until ten o'clock the next evening. No one awakened him to go on watch or disturbed him for meals. The crew respected each person's body rhythm, which told him when to eat and when to sleep, and so food and skins were always available.

When Lincoln finally woke up, he was refreshed and eager to help. He saw that the coffeepot was empty and busied himself making a brew as he had seen Kusiq and Tigluk do.

At midnight Kusiq woke up and asked Lincoln to go on watch with him. He was pleased to be asked. He liked Kusiq very much and hoped that this meant Kusiq liked him, too.

After fifteen minutes on watch Lincoln found it painful to stand absolutely still. He tried to concentrate his attention on the seals and gulls and ducks. He listened to the thunder talk of the ice and hummed diverting tunes when he was tempted to move. Vincent had said the length of a watch was up to each individual. Lincoln had set himself a goal of three hours.

Halfway into his watch, Kusiq waved his arm and pointed. On the other side of the lead a mother polar bear and two cubs walked slowly over the pack ice, the massive archipelago of ice that drifts around the North

Pole. The mother glided along as smoothly as a skater. Lincoln's heartbeat quickened. She was enormous, long necked, long torsoed and pale yellow against the white ice. Her eyes and nose were three black spots in the near distance. She walked to the edge of the water and, swinging her head from side to side as if talking to her cubs, dove in. The cubs, who were almost as big as she, followed.

The three came up in a line and swam swiftly without splashing. Lincoln was so fascinated, he did not notice that they were swimming his way. Kusiq did. He lifted his gun just as an ice floe passed between the bears and the boys. Although he could no longer see them, Kusiq kept his gun to his shoulder for a long time. The bears did not reappear.

An hour later soft-footed Ernie, Vincent's cousin, who Bertha said was famous for his whalebone carvings, came up behind Lincoln and tapped his shoulder. Lincoln was grateful. He trudged stiffly back to the tent, stomping his feet and shaking his hands.

"What did you see?" Vincent Ologak asked as Lincoln made himself a peanut-butter sandwich.

"Hundreds and hundreds of eider ducks, some seals and a polar bear with two cubs."

"That's pretty good. There was also a walrus and one lonely bowhead."

"A whale? And I missed him?"

"It is all right. We could not hunt him. He was too far out in the lead. If we had harpooned him, he would have dived under the pack ice and we would have lost him. A whale that is struck and gets away is counted the same as a landed whale. Barrow would have only three chances left. We must be sure we get the whales we hunt."

"You saw him?" Lincoln asked.

Vincent Ologak nodded.

"A bowhead whale," Lincoln said softly. "AġviQ was within yards of me. A great huge whale, and I didn't see him?"

"You will get new eyes out here all right," Vincent Ologak said. "Take a sleep."

A few hours later Lincoln awoke with a start.

"Ologak camp, this is Barrow. Do you copy?" He rolled onto his elbow.

[46]

Bertha was operating the CB. "I copy you, Barrow," she said, and switched to the receiver. While a woman talked excitedly in Iñupiat, Bertha and Vincent Ologak hugged each other and clapped their hands.

"Point Hope has just telephoned Barrow," Vincent translated. "They have landed a whale. Praise the Lord." His face was alive and as animated as if he had just heard the most wonderful news in the world. He found his parka and pulled it on.

"Come, Lincoln Noah," he said. "Come with me." Quickly, Lincoln dressed and followed.

Vincent Ologak walked with shuffling steps, his legs bowing at the knees as he crossed the ice to the umiaq. There he looked quietly out to sea, then beckoned to Lincoln.

"Listen closely, Lincoln Noah," he said. "Listen closely.

"For two years the people of Barrow have not gotten a whale. We have suffered. We have not been able to share. The Eskimo has survived by sharing. It is our first commandment—the religion before the Christians came. Sharing is born within us as the tusks are born in the walrus. We cannot share chicken and hamburger with all the people. It takes a whale to share."

Vincent Ologak slipped a paddle from its upright position in the boat and passed it to Lincoln.

"Your father said you are a strong paddler," he said. "You and I go out on the water to begin next year's whaling season. Like the summer sun, whaling is constant. As one season gets under way, we begin the next.

[47]

We need the bearded seal to cover next year's umiaq. The hides will be rolled and put in the ice cellar to freeze. In the winter Bertha will soak the skins in the ocean and I—or you—will scrape them clean. Scraping is a man's job. The women will select and sew them together."

The whaling captain walked to the crack in the ice where Utik had placed the sticks. The crack was no wider, but the sticks were no longer opposite each other—they were five yards apart.

"These sticks tell me the ice we are on is moving. The movement is not serious yet. Chunks break off here on the floating ice and sweep out to sea on the currents."

Vincent Ologak picked up a handful of snow and tossed it into the air. The wind blew it toward the southwest.

"The wind is right. We are safe for now." He gestured, and Lincoln helped him skid the umiaq into the water, then waited for the next command. Vincent folded his arms and stood beside him.

"Lincoln Noah," he said, "I have something very important to say to you." His eyes were soft, and his strength seemed to have returned.

"A whale is coming to you."

"A whale is coming to me, Vincent Ologak? I do not understand."

"The animals give themselves to the Eskimos. They let us kill them. They then become us: our blood, our voices, our spirits. They join us in our bodies. That is what they wish. We are all one."

Lincoln tried to understand. Vincent continued.

"When your father left my iglu many years ago, he asked me what he could do to thank me. And so I said to him: Name your first son Lincoln, for the great protector of men. And give him a second name Noah, for the great protector of animals."

"He never told me that," Lincoln said. "I sure wish he had. I always hated my name. Kids made fun of it." He paused. "I guess I never asked about it."

"Lincoln Noah is a fine name all right. I knew someday there would be a whale who would come to one named Lincoln Noah. I have waited and waited for you to grow up and the whale to grow old."

Lincoln looked down at his paddle. "That's hard for me to believe, Vincent Ologak," he said.

Vincent peered at him over his blue-rimmed sunglasses.

"The whale's name is Nukik—meaning strength in Iñupiat. He has a white scar across his back near his blowhole. His great flukes are all white.

"For two years he has passed close to me; but he did not want me to take him. He was waiting for you, Nora Ologak's great-great-grandson."

Lincoln was trying to take all this in when Tigluk ambled up and placed himself beside Vincent Ologak. He folded his arms on his chest as if he were a bodyguard, rose up and down on his toes, then wandered away.

"I don't think Tigluk likes me," said Lincoln.

"Tigluk is all right. He is good whale spotter," Vincent replied. "He can see whales through the fog. Sometimes he acts tough, and he can be pretty mean when he drinks. But he will not drink. No one is permitted to drink at whale camp. This is sacred work.

"Now we get into the umiaq."

Lincoln adjusted his gun.

"Leave your gun. I will shoot. Only Eskimos may shoot the marine mammals."

Willingly Lincoln leaned his rifle against an ice block, stepped into the umiaq and sat down. Paddling was not a new experience for him. He and Uncle Jack had canoed many eastern rivers; but this was an umiaq, made of skins and wooden slats, and he was leery of it. When Vincent was ready to get in, he kneeled on the bottom and grabbed the gunwales to steady the fragile boat. He did not have to. The umiaq was as stable as a rock. It barely moved when the whaling captain stepped in.

"A whale is coming to me," Lincoln said to himself, and was both perplexed and delighted.

The boat skimmed swiftly and lightly over the icy water with the balance of a leaf on a pond. Nevertheless, Lincoln was careful. He was not on Maine's Allagash or Vermont's Green River, but on the Arctic Ocean. He leaned into his work with utmost care.

Tigluk watched them paddle out toward the pack ice. When the umiaq was as big as a duck in the distance, he ambled over to Lincoln's gun, pulled open the chamber and removed the cartridge.

FOUR

Tigluk

THREE HOURS LATER Vincent and Lincoln returned to whale camp with one bearded seal for the umiaq and a ringed seal for Bertha. Her boots, Vincent had noticed, were worn thin on the bottoms, and patches of fur had been rubbed off.

Ernie and smiling Waldo came down to the water's edge to help with the umiaq. Upon seeing two seals, they lifted their voices in song and sang praises to ugruk, the bearded seal, and natchiQ, the ringed seal. Theirs was an ancient reception for a successful hunter, but Vincent did not linger. He was tired. After checking the crack in the ice, he left the three to pull the umiaq up on the ramp and haul the almost-frozen seals to the tent.

Lincoln put the seal-pulling rope over his shoulder and tugged. "A whale is coming to me," he said to himself. "Vincent Ologak says a whale is coming to me. Does Vincent say this to keep the whalers from harming me? Does he say this so I will be accepted out here? Whales do not come to people, and they certainly don't ask to be killed. There must be another reason for Vincent Ologak to tell me this."

He found Kusiq loading the sled with dead CB batteries and empty gasoline and kerosene cans.

"Are you going to Barrow, Kusiq?" Lincoln asked hopefully.

"I am," he answered, peering at the sun, which was a white glow in a shroud of pale-green ice fog that was rising off the open lead.

"Can I go with you?"

"Vincent Ologak needs you today," Kusiq replied. "The village of Wainwright has landed a whale. The whales are coming to Barrow. He needs you." Lincoln was surprised to hear Kusiq tell him he was needed—as far as Lincoln was concerned, he was just what a whaling camp did not need: a tanik, and an inexperienced boy tanik at that.

"Vincent Ologak's crew is small," Kusiq explained. "We have only eight men, including two apprentices— you and me. Most camps have ten or twelve men and three or four apprentices."

"But Vincent Ologak is a famous whaler," exclaimed Lincoln. "I'd think everyone would want to be on his crew."

"Whaling captains pay for the food and equipment. One snowmobile costs about four thousand dollars up here. Ten thousand dollars barely covers the cost of setting up a whale camp.

"And it is all spent for the people. No money is made on a whale."

"None?" Lincoln was surprised to hear this.

"The whale is a gift from the sea for everyone—the rich and poor, the old and sick. We cannot sell it." Kusiq seemed horrified at the thought of making money off a whale.

"We are a small crew because Vincent's health forced him to resign as mayor. He can afford only a few men. But we are the best." He threw out his chest and smiled proudly.

"With me among you?"

"You are important," he said, pulling his sunglasses down on his nose and looking over them at Lincoln. "A whale is coming to you, Lincoln Noah." He read Lincoln's doubting face. "This is a truth. Vincent Ologak says so. You must believe it. You stay in camp."

Lincoln's hope of finding Uncle Jack was dashed again. As time had passed, it had become apparent that Vincent Ologak was not going to talk about Jack James, so Lincoln had thought of another source of information. When his jet had been circling Barrow for a landing, the pilot had flipped on the intercom.

"If you'll look down to the right," he had said, "you'll see three clusters of tents near the open water. That is science camp. Men in that bleak outpost are counting bowhead whales as they migrate. They are funded by the Eskimos and the state of Alaska to determine just how many whales there are left and if the Eskimo can keep on whaling.

"Those guys have the most modern equipment available—hydrophones, computers, intercom radios, theodolites—but they live like Eskimos on the ice; tents, parkas, knee boots, sleeping bags, no modern conveniences. Take a run out there if you can. You'll understand the Arctic and the bowhead controversy—to whale or not to whale.

"Thank you for flying Alaska Airlines."

Lincoln had thought no more about science camp until he had realized Kusiq was going to town. Maybe the scientists would know where Uncle Jack was. They must know him. He was a whale scientist, too.

"I'd sure like to go with you, Kusiq," Lincoln persisted. His friend did not answer. He had made his statement.

Finally Lincoln took a self-addressed postcard his father had given him out of his snow shirt. On it he had written:

Dear Dad,
Having a good time. Tell Mom I have a delicious recipe for duck soup. I like my crazy name.
LNW.

"Kusiq, would you mail this for me?"

Kusiq, glad to oblige, pulled the starter cord and shot off into the whiteness, leaving Lincoln alone and wondering if he would ever find Uncle Jack.

He caught up with Vincent Ologak standing quietly at the edge of the crack, studying the ice and water.

"The air is still," the whaling captain said. "That is good. But the sea current is strong. It is bringing in siku, the pack ice."

"Pack ice?"

"The pack ice is permanent ice. It drifts around the

[54]

pole all year. It comes and goes. In the spring whaling season it hits the pan ice and smashes it into mountains called pressure ridges. It can also go out on the strong sea currents. Then it opens the leads for aġviQ." He stood very still staring at the lead. "Now siku is moving in." Lincoln could see no motion on the far side of the lead at all. He saw only flat, dark water and the unending ice that capped the top of the world.

Waldo and Tigluk joined them. When a whaling captain studies the ice as long as Vincent was, it is serious business. Pack ice is a two-headed monster that lives out in the ocean. One head is helpful, the other is destructive.

"If the wind does not blow from the northeast soon and push siku out," Vincent Ologak said to his crew, "we move camp."

"Move?" Lincoln thought of all the gear—tent, boat, sleds, food, stoves, radios.

"Whale hunters move often," Waldo said, then blew his breath into his ruff. The air was damp and felt much colder than it really was, although it was cold enough. It penetrated the seams in boots and clothing. Waldo warmed his toes by putting one boot toe on top of the other and then reversing the procedure.

"The ice is very dangerous," Vincent Ologak went on, directing his words to Lincoln. "You must learn about it. The first rule is never to go out on the new ice when a mild wind blows from the south, a small new south wind.

"And never go out on the new ice if there are narrow clouds everywhere.

"When it gets that way, the ice will be taken away—very fast.

"If that happens to you, if the ice you are on goes out, run against the direction it is moving. You will come to a bridge of ice or a pan. Hop on it. Float yourself across the narrow spot, or swim. Otherwise you will be carried out to sea."

Lincoln listened with ears, eyes and brain.

"Long ago," Vincent mused, "after I became aware, I drifted out on an ice floe with my father's whaling crew. We drifted 200 miles, I guess, out of sight for a long time. We got seals and cooked them by making fires right on them with their blubber. We got a polar bear and used the skin for the bottoms of our boots so they wouldn't wear out and freeze us.

"The wind changed, and we came in sight of land. We saw Inianniik, the hills southeast of Barrow that look like a woman's breasts.

"We pulled our boat to the edge of our ice floe, pushed off and paddled to shore. We had spent more than a month out there. I cried when I felt the land again."

This siku, Lincoln thought, was truly a force to be reckoned with. He looked at the pack ice and then the tent.

"Why do you camp in such danger, Vincent Ologak?"

"To be near the lead edges to hunt. Also, whales are big and heavy. We must be almost level with the water to pull them in. You will see." He picked up a shovel and a spear that were lying near the umiaq.

"Come with me, Lincoln Noah," Vincent Ologak said,

and he walked polar-bear-footed over the new ice that had formed on the quiet water during the dusk of midnight. Lincoln followed, walking like a polar bear, too.

In this manner they reached Tigluk, who had taken the watch on the south perch.

"Qasuaq pilik," the young man called to Vincent Ologak, pointedly excluding Lincoln from the conversation.

"Bad calm all right," Vincent translated, letting Lincoln in. "But the pack ice is coming in slowly. The winds may change." Lincoln searched the sky for the narrow clouds the whaling captain had warned about. There were none.

Vincent Ologak walked on. Lincoln followed him around a massive green-blue block of ice wedged into the floating ice not far from the spot where Vincent had killed the ringed seal. After a short hike they stopped before a mountain of powder blue ice almost twenty feet high.

"Pressure ridge," Vincent said. "This is what happens when the siku closes the leads and hits the new ice where we are camped. Mountains pile up. Before that happens, we go. Whalers read the ice and sky and winds and heed their warnings."

"What brings siku in?"

"The current and a southwest wind. Keep throwing up snow when you are on watch. Tell me always which way the wind blows all right."

They clambered up the pressure ridge, Vincent stopping now and then to catch his breath. On the other side he poked his spear into drifts of snow. Not finding what he was seeking, he moved on. Presently he squatted, sniffed the snow and pushed back his parka hood to listen. Swiftly he stuck the spear into a large drift. This time he hit a hole and the spear went in without resistance.

Digging with his shovel, Vincent Ologak opened a skylight into a turquoise-blue room.

"Seal iglu," he said.

The seal had chewed a plunge hole up through the ice into the snowdrift and had carved out the room with nose and flippers. She kept the plunge hole open by constantly biting and chewing at it, for here she slept and ate her Arctic cod after a hunt, and here she gave birth.

Vincent Ologak poked his head and shoulders far down into the room, inhaled deeply and grunted with satisfaction.

"Natchiagruk, baby seal." His smile was so wide that his back molars shone. "I smell him," he said excitedly, and dug the hole larger.

"Go down, Lincoln Noah." He pointed into the den. "The ringed seal we killed was a nursing mother. Her pup cannot get out of his den. Last night while he waited for her to return, the plunge hole froze solid. Go down and get the baby seal, Lincoln Noah."

Vincent Ologak seemed to have no doubts about Lincoln's climbing into the seal iglu, and so, without more than a brief hesitation, he slid in. He had done crazier things than this in his life, like the day he had gone down into a cave on a rope to look for a treasure. A deep pool of water had lain at the bottom, and he had been forced to climb right back up without resting.

The domed seal cave, which was high enough to crawl around in on hands and knees, was powder blue in color and lit by the sun that was shining through the snow and Vincent's hole. Along the wall were rounded niches where the mother seal had rested. Her warm body had shaped the snow. The walls of the cave glistened with green ice, the frozen moisture from the seal's breathing. It had insulated the den, keeping it well above zero—almost comfortable, Lincoln thought.

"Wow, Vincent Ologak," he called. "I could live here all right." Vincent peered down at him.

"Do you see the natchiagruk—the infant seal?" he asked.

A tunnel led off into the snowbank. Lincoln crawled along it to a dark room against a block of ice. He blinked. Two large black eyes in a round white face were looking at him. Lincoln sucked in his breath at the sight of such innocence and beauty.

"Will he bite?" he called up to Vincent.

"He does not bite. Bring him up, Lincoln Noah. He cannot live without our help."

The infant animal did not struggle when Lincoln put his hands around his hard strong body and drew him to his chest.

"NatchiQ," he whispered, "forgive me." Lincoln smiled at himself. Yesterday when Vincent Ologak had killed the mother, he had bared his white head, bowed, and asked the spirit of the dead seal for forgiveness. Now here he was, Lincoln Noah Stonewright of New Bedford, Massachusetts, asking a baby seal to forgive him for his

part in the death of his mother. Apologies for victory in the battle of survival in the Arctic seemed to come instinctively. He hugged the little seal to himself and climbed into the sunlight.

The flippers of the baby sea mammal spun in the air, and his funny back feet flapped like Charlie Chaplin's, fused at the heels. Vincent Ologak spoke softly to him in Iñupiat. The words were soothing, like a snow bunting's song, and the little fellow relaxed and snuggled against Lincoln's body.

"What are you going to do with him?" Lincoln asked with naked concern. He had fallen in love with the beautiful natchiQ.

"Take care of him until he can fend for himself. Then we'll let him go," Vincent answered. "We do not need him. Annie has all the baby-seal fur she needs for clothing. We have plenty of meat. I do not kill the animals we do not need."

"Oh, good," Lincoln said, blowing through his lips in relief. He could eat duck soup and caribou stew, but not this charming sea person. Smiling thankfully at Vincent, he tucked NatchiQ under his parka and tightened his belt to hold him there. Happily he followed his whaling captain back to camp, watching for thin clouds and feeling the stillness.

Tigluk was coming off watch. Lincoln took the baby out of his parka and held him up for him to admire.

"Isn't he cute, Tigluk?" he called.

"Yum, yum. Let's eat him." Tigluk slipped his knife from its sheath on his belt as Vincent Ologak approached him from behind.

"None of that, Tigluk," Vincent Ologak said like a father reprimanding a small child. The young man smirked and put his knife away.

"Lincoln Noah," the whaling captain went on, "dig little NatchiQ a cave in the snowdrift by the tent. And ask Bertha to give you a frozen fish. NatchiQ is old enough to eat fish all right. If you feed him, he will think you are his mother and follow you like a dog."

The expedition had tired Vincent. He patted NatchiQ and went into the tent to rest.

Tigluk looked from right to left. Ernie and Waldo were on watch with their backs turned. No one else was present. He sneaked up behind Lincoln and put his mouth to his ear.

"Taniks get pushed off the ice," he warned. "Watch your step."

[61]

Lincoln heard, decided not to react and, dropping to his knees, began scooping out a cave for NatchiQ. He had never experienced racism before. It hurt and was demeaning, and it was very scary. He hugged the baby seal for comfort.

Several hours later he relieved Ernie, who reported to him that he had seen no whales, that the air was motionless and the lead was somewhat smaller, but not alarmingly so. The north wind might yet come and blow the pack ice away.

As he stood above the water, an eeriness settled upon the ice world. Lincoln did not understand the atmosphere, and it made him feel very uneasy. He wondered what had created the mood: Was it the stillness, was it Tigluk? Wherever it came from, it was chilling. He glanced down at the crack. The land-side sticks lay where they had been placed. The lead-side ones, however, had rotated yards closer to the lead. The ice on which they were camped was breaking off.

When his watch was over, he went into the tent and reported this to Vincent, who beckoned to Utik as he stepped outside. Vincent Ologak tossed snow and squinted at the sky. He measured the distance of the incoming pack ice by holding up his thumb at arm's length and counting the number of times it would fit between the pack ice and the edge of lead where they stood.

"Time to go?" Utik asked.

"There is still no southwest wind to blow siku in. There are still no narrow clouds. We are not yet in trouble. A wind may yet come from the north. It often does under these conditions." He rocked up on his toes and pushed his hands up into his sleeves.

"Weir Amaogak will soon be here," he continued. "He's coming along the coast from Wainwright. He will note things along the way. Also, Bertha asked him to stop at the weather station and look over the satellite images. We may know more when he gets here. We may know less. That is how it is."

"What does the CB weather reporter say?"

"That the leads from Point Hope to Wainwright are closed—that one whale puddle is open forty miles west of Barrow and that Adam's crew east of the point radioed to say the pack ice is about to hit."

"We ought to get off the ice."

"This is a good spot: south of the point. The current is flowing south. It will hold our lead open and our ice in place. We will stay longer. Nukik will come to this lead."

Utik said no more. His captain had spoken.

"Nukik has passed Wainwright. He is headed our way." Vincent Ologak's eyes narrowed. "For some reason, I know this."

"Nukik is coming our way?" Utik asked eagerly. "How big did you say he is?"

"Fifty feet—fifty tons."

"Lotsa maktak."

"Lotsa maktak."

Lincoln, returned to the umiaq perch, a broad platform

[63]

about five feet high, blew his breath into his wolverine fur, put his feet close together and scanned the now-purple water. He did not see Tigluk walk to the far side of the umiaq and sit down.

When Sagniq relieved him, Lincoln hurried to NatchiQ's den. The baby came sliding out to meet him, moving along with his flippers and the buckling motions of his land-awkward body. Lincoln laughed, gathered him up in his arms and took him into the tent. Bertha was cracking frozen carrots with a knife handle. She stopped her work to get a fish from the frigid edge of the tent and offered it to the beautiful baby.

"I just love him," she said, and stroked his smooth head. "He reminds me of my grandchildren—so bright-eyed and pretty."

NatchiQ was, indeed, a personality. He was tear shaped, lively and bursting with energy. He liked people. Even sober Ernie's face crinkled happily at the sight of the baby seal. Lincoln held NatchiQ in his lap. The natchiagruk's flippers whirled like little windmills, and his hind feet patted Lincoln's lap as he fed him the fish.

When NatchiQ was satiated, he snuggled down in Lincoln's arms, closed his large, glistening eyes and went to sleep. Lincoln tucked him into the skins and offered to peel onions for Bertha.

"We never used veggies when I grew up," she said. "When the stuaqpak came to town, the manager had these silly things shipped up from outside."

"They're good for you," Lincoln said.

"I am not so sure. I grew very strong on seal liver and maktak. My granddaughter who eats veggies is not so strong." Lincoln thought about the traditional Eskimo foods he had been eating. Out here in the cold he actually relished them. They gave him more quick energy than candy, and he could stay up long hours and work hard. Maybe Bertha's doubts about vegetables were well-founded up here.

When he was finished with chipping the skins off the frozen onions, he went outside and checked the crack. The sticks were still rotating apart, but more slowly. He returned and scrubbed a pot for Bertha, then swept the floor where the pinochle players sat.

"It's fun to be a whaling apprentice," he said to Bertha; then quickly added, "But don't tell my mother."

Bertha laughed and promised she would never repeat what he had said.

"Vincent should get up and check the ice again," Bertha said, glancing at her husband. "But he is sleeping so well, I do not like to wake him. He does not sleep well lately."

"Can I do it?" Lincoln offered.

"Tell me if there are any thin clouds. That's all we need to know."

Lincoln carried NatchiQ to his den and circled the tent to get a complete view of the sky.

"Nothing but blue, blue sky," he reported. "Even the fog is gone."

"Hmmmm," said Bertha, and glanced at her husband.

Lincoln picked up his gun and went out to relieve Sagniq.

"The sticks are still rotating apart," Sagniq reported. "But all is well." Then he added, "Except no whales are coming by."

An hour into the watch an enormous flock of eider ducks flew around Lincoln for almost five minutes without letup. He could hear their wings thrumming and see the golden shields on the beaks of the males. The birds dodged him as if he were just another piece of ice on the seascape. He reached out and almost caught one.

"Keep your eye on the lead!" It was Tigluk. He was hunkered down by the umiaq, carving a big piece of whalebone with a knife held in his bare hands. Lincoln looked back at the water.

Utik, who was also on watch, did not hear Tigluk's angry voice, for sounds do not carry far on the ice; and so no one saw Tigluk lean his gun against the umiaq and swagger up onto the perch. He tiptoed toward Lincoln.

"Tanik!"

Lincoln turned.

"Keep your eyes on the water." Tigluk snarled and spit. This time Lincoln did not obey. He was not going to turn his back on Tigluk. The sea was only a push away. He watched him come closer.

Then he saw the polar bear. It was on the perch behind Tigluk.

"Bear!" Lincoln yelled. Tigluk spun around and screamed in terror. He had no gun. He tried to get behind Lincoln.

Lincoln raised his rifle and pulled the trigger.

Click!

The bear snarled and lunged at Tigluk, and Lincoln raised his useless gun and brought it down with all his strength on the polar bear's nose. The gun stock splintered. The bear fell down. Quickly he staggered to his feet.

Tigluk wailed.

A shot rang out. The bear crumpled and dropped onto the ice. Utik ran up pumping his gun for another shot but did not need to take it. The bear was dead.

No one spoke for what seemed to be an entire lifetime to Lincoln. Finally Utik cleared his throat.

"You are a very strong boy," he said. "Tigluk was almost a spirit."

The shot brought Vincent, Bertha and Sagniq to the perch.

Vincent Ologak whispered an almost inaudible prayer for the bear, then leaned over the magnificent animal, whose red blood shone vividly on the white snow. He picked up a thick paw that was both wicked and charming. He lifted the black-rimmed lips and examined the teeth.

"It is a two-year-old. Must be one of the cubs Lincoln and Kusiq saw. They were big. The mother ran them off. This bear was very hungry. Beware of the other one."

Sagniq still could not speak. He looked from the bear to the broken rifle to his son. Finally, he found his voice.

"You saved Tigluk's life, Lincoln. I thank you."

Lincoln smiled weakly and picked up his broken gun. Bertha touched his arm gently.

"You just got yourself an Eskimo name all right." She touched the bear's massive head. "You are Karuk—hit-on-the-head."

"Karuk—I like that."

"Now you have two names—one English, one Iñupiat. That makes you an Eskimo all right."

"I like that, too."

"Some Eskimo boy all right," Utik said. "Karuk is strong all right."

Bertha leaned over and apologized to the bear, then hurried to the tent to tell the story of Karuk to the Eskimo CB audience.

It took Ernie, Tigluk and Utik to haul the five-hundred-pound cub to the tent to be dressed out. The fur would make a valuable rug as well as boots and mitten trim, and the meat would be made into stew.

Tigluk walked into the tent, his body trembling like aspen leaves. Lincoln and Vincent stood quietly on the ice perch. Lincoln studied the shattered gun stock, turning it over in his hands. Vincent touched his arm.

"You should have loaded your gun," he admonished in a gentle but firm voice.

"I did." Lincoln looked deep into Vincent's eyes and said no more.

"We sorely need a whale," Vincent Ologak said. "We sorely need a whale."

FIVE

Nukik

WEIR AMAOGAK was somewhere in the white barrens between Wainwright and Barrow, humming as he pulled his graceful basket sled with a borrowed snow machine. He was coming along the coast on his way to join the Vincent Ologak crew. He glanced back to check on his thirteen-year-old granddaughter, Ukpik. She was tucked in the furs on the old-style sled Weir had made of bent willow limbs from the foot of the Brooks Range. She sat with her feet straight out like a sitting bear's. Her nose and eyes peeked out of her blowing wolverine ruff. Weir Amaogak smiled to see his favorite person in all the world riding through the ice-bound wilderness with him. This was the second time he had taken her whaling, and he was glowing with thoughts of whales and this helpful grandchild.

Ukpik sat on a box that held Weir's harpoon, whale lance, ice saws and block and tackle. The harpooner had spent three weeks cleaning, sharpening and oiling the

equipment out of respect for the whale. Everything must be perfect for the perfect animal.

Weir Amaogak was the last traditional harpooner. He used a harpoon to which was attached a pre-white–man sealskin float. When the harpoon was embedded in the whale, the float brought the animal to the surface and slowed it down so Weir could take it mercifully and honorably with his lance. He did not use the modern harpoon and shoulder gun that are equipped with bombs, for Weir did not use modern equipment. He used his old and primitive tools, his own knowledge of the anatomy of whale and his strength. He never missed.

He was also one of the last Eskimos in the Arctic to own a dog team. He had borrowed a friend's snow machine for this trip, leaving his lively huskies at home out of consideration for his beloved friend Vincent Ologak. Dogs require a lot of food, and Vincent was no longer wealthy.

Also on the sled were survival supplies. The harpooner traveled his Arctic homeland with a stove, pots, food, gun, ammunition and skins. He carried these in the summer and winter, on five-hundred-mile trips as well as on two-mile excursions. He was alive because he took the same precautions his ancestors had taken when they traveled—he carried a home with him. No modern technology, which had changed so much of the North Slope and Eskimo life, could change the weather at the top of the world. As far as Weir was concerned, it was as dangerous and unpredictable as it had been when the Eskimos had migrated to the Arctic twenty thousand years ago.

Weir drove at a steady pace on the smooth ice along the beach. He noted the caribou on the land, the eider ducks out over the ice and, here and there, the graceful little Arctic foxes. This was a dangerous time for the foxes. It was spring, and they were anticipating the gray landscape of summer. Their fur was changing from white to gray. This, together with their black eyes and noses, made them more visible to enemies on the white snow and ice.

Weir checked on Ukpik again, and this time she pointed to her mouth to say she was hungry. Gladly he slowed down and stopped. He had been driving for many hours and was ready for a rest. He reached into a skin bag, brought out the paniqtaq—dried fish and seal meat—and carried it to her.

"How much longer?" she asked.

"Less than half a sleep to go."

She slid off the sled, stretched her arms and hopped up and down to exercise her legs and toes. Ukpik was a petite young lady whose small nose and large black eyes gave her the wondrous look of natchiagruk, the baby seal. Her skin was like golden silk, and her red cheeks knotted into little apples when she smiled. Ukpik was very beautiful.

Ukpik means snowy owl in Iñupiat. Although her English name was Patsy, she preferred to be called Little Owl, an affectionate name that Annie had given her.

Little Owl was studying her native tongue in school—unlike her mother, who had been forbidden to speak Iñupiat by her teachers. It was Annie who had changed this demeaning state of affairs. Almost single-handedly she had fought the whole U.S. Bureau of Indian Affairs school bureaucracy to have Iñupiat and Eskimo history taught in the North Slope villages. Her battle was won when Little Owl was born. As a consequence Little Owl was not ashamed, but fiercely proud of her heritage. She also studied English, mathematics and American and English history, and took a course in corporate law. This was in preparation for her dual way of life as an American citizen and an Eskimo. The native villages of Alaska are incorporated. They invest their percentage of the oil taken on their land and spend the profits on their people. Schoolchildren are given a hundred dollars apiece by the

North Slope School District to invest in their own school corporations. The children make and sell Eskimo doughnuts, charge for dances and invest the money they raise. Some graduate and manage the village corporations. Little Owl enjoyed her complicated education and was an excellent student.

She sat down on the snow machine beside Weir to finish her seal meat.

"What is Vincent Ologak's new apprentice like, Ataata?" she asked her grandfather.

"The what?"

"The new boyer, Vincent Ologak's relative from the outside? I heard you talking to Bertha about him."

"The new boyer. Yes, yes, that would interest you. I am getting old. Let me see, Bertha says he has not so much Eskimo in him and that he is very strong."

"Oh, Ataata, that's not what I'm asking. Did she say he was handsome? How old is he?"

"He is young. He is a piayaaq aġviQ—a whale who has just left his mother."

"I mean how many years, silly Ataata."

"So young that his blubber is soft, like a young whale's."

She stopped pursuing that subject. "Do you think he'll be angry with me?"

"Be angry with you? Why would he be?"

"Because I will be paddling the umiaq with you when you go out to harpoon the whale."

"Yes, I want you. You are a strong paddler. But why should the boyer care?"

"Well, don't you think a boyer from the lower forty-eight would resent that? Me, a girl, in the boat and him in the kitchen?"

"Oh, he will be in the boat all right. Vincent Ologak says Nukik, the whale, will give himself to this boy."

"Vincent Ologak said that?" Her eyes widened. "Then it must be so."

Weir Amaogak pushed back his parka hood to better see the frozen ocean. A thick cap of silver-gray hair tumbled around his face and neck. Bold lines ran from his nose to the corners of his mouth, calling attention to his broad full lips. The half-moon eyes were permanently squinted from a lifetime of watching the ice and the wildlife. He blew on his bare hands and studied the horizon.

"Water sky, Ukpik," he said. "Want to ride out and see if the whales are passing through that lead?"

"I love to watch whales."

"The second wave of whales is late. Maybe we can learn something."

Weir Amaogak unhitched the sled. Little Owl swung onto the backseat of the snow machine and hugged her grandfather around the waist. They started out across the land-fast shore ice that forms in coves and is smoother than the open-sea ice. In a short distance the ice roughened, and Weir was bumping the machine through valleys and over pressure ridges beyond the cove. The water sky grew darker and darker until it hung like a rainstorm above them.

"We are here," Weir said, pulling around a blue-green

ice mound and stopping beside a lake of open water in the continent of ice.

"Whale puddle," he said of the lake.

Its edges sparkled with a covering of thin clear ice that was forming in the calm. Weir studied the open water in the middle of the puddle while Little Owl observed the shores.

"AiviQ," she said, pointing to a monstrous brown walrus sitting like a pompous king on the edge of the whale puddle. His ivory tusks, which came down to the middle of his chest, were blunted by years of fighting bulls for his harem. The light gleamed on the wire-thick whiskers that jutted out of his puffy lips. He stared stone faced at Little Owl.

"Is he giving himself to us?" Ukpik asked. "He sits so still."

Weir did not answer. He was concentrating on the new ice near the east end of the whale puddle. Ukpik turned back to the walrus.

"Go home, aiviQ," she called. "We do not need you."

"Whale!" whispered Weir, pointing to a black slick at the far end of the lake. "AġviQ—see him?"

The slick moved and the black blowhole of an enormous whale lifted into the air.

Whoosssfff. The giant shot a geyser into the sun. Although Weir and Ukpik had seen hundreds and hundreds of whales, they watched as if this were their very first—in awed silence.

The whale went under, came up, breathed out and in,

went under again. He did this seven times, then he sounded—dived deep and stayed down for thirteen minutes.

The thin ice that had formed in front of Weir and Little Owl buckled up into a huge air-filled dome. A whale could be seen inside it taking a breath. Weir dropped onto his stomach. Little Owl lay down beside him. They waited. The whale vanished.

Presently it blew in the open water, then lifted itself up until its twenty-foot head was in view. It turned one eye on the man and the girl. Thrashing its flukes, it rose yet higher.

"Sky hopping!" Weir whispered. "That's higher than a breach. The whale is excited." Little Owl held her breath. The giant was no more than thirty feet away and as big as the Wainwright church. The profile of its mouth curved up, then down, and ended just below its thoughtful eye. Water poured out between the rows of baleen in the great smile. It stood on end for a long moment, then threw itself onto the new ice and shattered it. Pieces shot out in all directions like glass spears. They tinkled as they fell back. Green and purple waves rolled up from the fall, breaking more ice. The whale spiraled onto its belly and, with a graceful twist, put its head in the water. Its back came into view. A flipper whirled and the tail stock, which seems too narrow for the bowhead bulk, curved above the water. Slowly the huge flukes lifted. They were white.

"Nukik!" Weir said softly.

A chill ran down Little Owl's spine. The leviathan was, indeed, looking for someone. She had seen his humanlike eye scanning Weir, then herself. The intelligence behind it had been dissatisfied or perhaps not interested. Nukik, she knew in her heart, was searching for Vincent Ologak's camp and the boyer. The white teachers at school did not believe whales gave themselves to people.

Another whale surfaced and blew far out in the whale puddle, and close at hand a female with a baby at her side came up to breathe. The mother lifted her youngster to the surface with a flipper. He took a breath, peered around and saw Little Owl. He lifted his head higher

[77]

and wiggled his long gray-blue body, as if he knew another youngster when he saw one. Little Owl clapped her mittens over her mouth to keep from crying out in glee. The baby splashed and waved its flippers; then the mother scooped him up and dove with him. They left whale tracks, great swathes of smooth water on the surface outlined with turbulent bubbles.

"Oh, Ataata," Little Owl whispered. "I wish I could swim under the water with them. We land creatures can never really know the whales—only their blowholes and tails."

"Perhaps I can help you, Little Owl," Weir said, getting to his feet. "I sometimes feel that I am part whale, as Annie thinks she is part wolf. Sit down, little granddaughter. I will tell you what Nukik is doing.

"The water where he swims is green. Spears of gold light come down from the top of the water. They are the glowing lamps that lead Nukik to air. He looks for these bright guides that tell him where the leads are when he travels under the ice. It is pretty in Nukik's world. Fish flash around him, the ice shines, the kelp on the bottom of the sea dances and reaches up to him.

"The mother and baby have followed Nukik to the east end of the puddle. They are resting now." Weir sat very still, waiting for Nukik to do something else.

"Nukik is leading them under the ice."

Seven minutes passed without Weir speaking.

"Nukik has found a crack in the ice beyond the puddle, and the mother and baby are breathing there. They hang at the surface. They are comfortable and safe.

"Nukik is listening to the ice and current. He learns from the screeching of ice against ice that the leads are closed for miles and miles ahead. He and his pod of friends and relatives cannot travel their ancestral route along the shore." Weir suddenly smiled.

"Close your eyes, Little Owl. Can you see Nukik? He is very big and very fat. His head is slightly pointed. White scars mark his black skin. He is pocked with many holes and bumps. He is an old whale.

"He must be my age, Little Owl. Whales are like people. They have a long childhood, and like people they don't have babies until they are in their teens. They grow wise and old like us, and some, like some people, become good leaders. Nukik is one of these.

"And like us, whales grow old and die. Nukik's life is run. He is ready to complete the cycle and live again in our spirits and our bodies." Weir's voice was reverent and low.

"Much of this knowledge I know from my father and grandfather, who learned it from their fathers and grandfathers as far back as there have been Eskimo whalers. And I have added some new knowledge of my own."

"The whales must know about the Eskimos," Little Owl said. "Do you think, Ataata?"

"They probably know a lot about us," answered Weir. "And they probably know individual Eskimos as we know individual whales. I have seen Nukik of the white fluke many times. I am sure he knows me. One spring I saw him off Point Hope, when I harpooned for Ernie Fellow. Nukik waved a flipper. Last spring I saw him when I was with Vincent Ologak. He sky hopped for us, but he would not give himself to us. We were not the person he was looking for."

Weir stopped talking and read the sun as if it were a clock in the sky. He started the snow machine and drove back to the sled. Little Owl did not get on it.

"Don't go yet, Ataata," she said. "Nukik and his friends are in trouble. Please tell me what he is doing now."

Life in the Arctic cannot be rushed, as every Eskimo knows, so Weir sat down. Passing on knowledge to the young is the most important thing an elder can do, and Weir took his responsibilities seriously.

He closed his eyes.

"Nukik has left the mother and baby resting in the crack. He pumps his whole body up and down and swims under the pack ice. He is watching for the lamps in the gloom. He sees only purple darkness, and far behind him the glow of the whale puddle like a moonrise under the sea."

Little Owl felt as if she were under the water at last. She closed her eyes.

"Now Nukik uses his senses. He hears the cracks and tastes the air pockets. They taste of sun. He finds an area where there are many cracks.

"Ahead is a mountain range of pack ice that reaches almost down to the ocean floor. It is jagged in some places, smooth in others. It is yellow and blue and green. The water pressure tells Nukik that the barrier goes on and on. The baby cannot dive deep enough to get under it or hold its breath long enough to find the air pockets.

"Nukik takes his kind of compass reading on this location. He photographs the shapes on his brain and notes the taste of the water. He returns to his pod and leads them to the breathing cracks under the pack ice. Now he returns to the mother and baby."

Apparently there was a lull in the events in the ocean, for Weir was silent. Little Owl thought of a question while they waited.

"Where did Nukik come from?" she asked.

"In the winter Nukik and his pod live with the sun in a secret place in the Bering Sea. Almost two weeks ago the lengthening day and the warming waters told them it was time to migrate to their summer home. They swam east with the second wave of a thousand or more whales.

"The first wave is made up of adolescents and young adults. They left the Bering Sea in early April and are now in their summering grounds. The third wave, of assorted sizes and ages, will pass Barrow in late May and early June.

"Nukik's wave is made up of mothers, their babies and youngsters, pregnant females and old whales like himself. Why the whales break up into these waves is known only to the whales.

"Nukik's wave swam until they came to the Bering Straits. There they were stopped by an ice jam that blocked the narrow pass.

"They were delayed many days. Finally, the sun warmed

the water, the ice jam melted and floated away and Nukik and his pod continued. They swam past the Point Hope whalers without giving themselves. They swam by the Wainwright whalers without giving themselves and were stopped today by that wall of pack ice. So happily we came upon them." Weir's eyes opened and closed again. "Nukik is active."

"What is he doing now, Ataata?"

"He is circling the mother and baby. He slows down, for he hears something. He listens. A walrus is calling; his voice sounds like a church bell ringing underwater. The walrus is on his way to the bottom to dig in the mud for clams. Seals are whistling like chirruping birds. One shoots up from the depths, passes Nukik and pops up into her blue iglu. But now he is not listening for walrus and seals.

"Nukik usually pays attention to the seals. They feed on the fish that feed on the plankton. By joining the seals he finds the plankton.

"He also listens for the chirps of the beluga whales. They, too, eat the fish that feed on the plankton. But these voices do not interest him now." Weir cocked his head to one side, and the creases in his dark face smoothed as he concentrated.

"Nukik is listening for the voice of a bowhead, a deep lugubrious moo. He heard it once. He knows who it is, and the whale's call is urgent."

Little Owl clasped her hands together.

"Ataata, what is happening?"

"Nukik is back to the whale puddle. He finds the whale. She is a pregnant female. Nukik sounds, swims toward her and with grace breaches and looks around.

"There is no midwife or attendant with the female. Whales need help with their newborns. A friend usually lifts the baby to air as soon as it is born and while the mother recovers.

"Most whales are born in the water, but this mother throws her tail up on a thick piece of new ice. Her abdomen contracts with great force. Nukik sky hops, rising to the base of his tail stock. The female gives a long, low moo and delivers a fifteen-foot baby onto the ice."

"A baby whale has been born? Ataata, how lovely." Little Owl leaned closer, for Weir's eyes were scrunched tight and his voice was low.

"The infant snorts air, and the mother gently nudges him into the sea with her tail. She holds him up on her flipper to breathe. She lets him sink. She lifts him up. She lets him sink. At last the baby has learned the rhythm of breathing. Nukik swims quietly up to the little whale.

"He noses his granddaughter affectionately."

"Ataata, Ataata." Little Owl clapped her hands. "Nukik has a granddaughter. She will be good to him and love him." Weir squeezed Little Owl's hands and got to his feet. He glanced at the sun, then back at his granddaughter.

"Nukik will not lead his pod on. They will swim east without him. Nukik will stay with his daughter and granddaughter and the other mother and baby. He will teach them about the sea. He will breach and splash for them.

"And then, when the shore leads open again, Nukik will lead them to Vincent Ologak's camp. There he will leave them forever."

SIX

Sagvaq, the current Anugl, the wind

WHALE CAMP was quiet when Weir and Little Owl tiptoed into aullaagvik the next day pulling their beautiful sled behind them. Lincoln and Ernie, who were on watch, did not hear their footsteps, they fell so softly. With the silence of owl wings Ukpik slipped into the tent with the sleepers, and Weir went to the umiaq. He removed Vincent's modern bomb harpoon, its nylon rope and its pink plastic float, and replaced them with his own. His harpoon had been made out of a walrus jawbone by his great-grandfather and was polished to the smoothness of glass. The shaft was tapered to ride true through the air. On the top of it was an ivory toggle point on a shaft. It slid out of a groove in the shaft when the mark was hit. To the toggle point was attached one end of a rope of intricately twisted walrus hide. To the other end was tied the sealskin float that pops to the surface when the whale is struck and marks its position. Like all Weir's equipment, the sealskin float was a design of the past. It

was a whole seal with flippers and hind feet intact and the fur scraped off to leave a fine tough skin. Blown up, it looked like a stuffed toy.

In place of the shoulder bomb Weir laid down a bone lance tipped with a gorgeous spearhead of jade. Weir was not sure where it had come from. A family story recounted some travelers from Asia who had traded with Weir's forebears, exchanging the jade for walrus ivory.

Weir arranged his treasures with great care. His tools must not only be clean and beautiful, but be placed precisely right, again out of respect for the great whale.

When he was satisfied, he walked to the edge of the lead and folded his arms. Lincoln turned and saw the famous harpooner for the first time. He was broad of build and short in stature, and like Vincent Ologak he held his back straight, his head high. He was different from any Eskimo Lincoln had seen. His snow shirt was not white nylon, like everyone else's, but sealskin scraped to the whiteness and softness of cloth. His knee-highs were sealskin crisscrossed with thongs, and he wore polar-bear slippers. His sunglasses were made of driftwood with two slits carved in them. Weir did not need a store. The Arctic provided all his needs.

Vincent Ologak was awakened by the soft sounds of Little Owl putting down her caribou skin and furs. Everyone else was asleep in the tent, even Bertha. Lying very still, with his eyes open, his white hair pushed back from his broad forehead, Vincent Ologak watched Little Owl. How happy her presence made him feel. His old friend Weir must think a great deal of Vincent to bring his dearest possession to his whale camp.

Vincent Ologak and Weir Amaogak were free-thinking leaders, and although most whalers did not have women in camp, not even wives although they were the managers in town, he and Weir found them to be a definite attribute. And that settled that.

When Little Owl had curled into her furs and closed her eyes, Vincent struggled to his feet.

Bertha woke up when he moved. She rolled over and looked at her husband in surprise. He was moving with more agility than he had shown in months. He fairly ran out of the tent.

Weir opened his arms, Vincent opened his arms and the two men fell together. They hugged strongly, slapping each other's backs and laughing.

"It's been too long since we got a whale," Vincent said.

"Too long all right," replied Weir. "Our people have suffered. This year we will make everything all right."

"My sister-in-law," Vincent said, "will stop stealing stored maktak from my sister. And my sister will stop hating herself for hating her sister-in-law for stealing."

"My brother," said Weir, "will stop arguing with his wife, and his wife will stop picking on him."

"And those people of Barrow who hate taniks will like them. When we do not have a whale, we do not behave right." Vincent gazed dreamily at the sea. "We are getting old, Weir Amaogak," he went on softly. "Do you think we can do it?"

"Oh, we can do it all right. Remember the whale you and I got by ourselves, just we two?"

Vincent nodded. "You killed him with your great-grandfather's lance, nicely and instantly. We pushed him along the ice bank in the fog for seven miles until we came to a camp for help to land him. We were then only piayaaqs, aġviQs who had just left their mothers, like these children." He gestured toward Lincoln, who was still on watch, and Kusiq, who had just returned from Barrow and was unloading supplies.

"But we did it all right." They felt joy in the bottoms of their bellies, these two cozy elders of the ice.

Even while they reminisced, Weir was taking note of the position of Vincent's camp on the last open lead south of the point. He was pleased.

"I saw Nukik," he said, getting down to business.

Vincent's face grew peaceful. "You saw old Nukik?"

"He's coming your way all right."

"He'll come to us," Vincent agreed. "I still have enough strength to paddle you right up to him. You step up on his back like the old days and drive the lance true."

"I'm not so good at that anymore, Vincent Ologak," Weir replied. "I stay in the boat these days. I am a grandfather."

"And I am a grandfather, too, and a great-grandfather; but we have many years of experience behind us. That is better than strength."

"Where is the boyer?"

"He is the one on the far perch."

"A little pale," Weir said, catching a glimpse of Lincoln's forehead.

"But he's a good one," said Vincent Ologak. "He felled a bear with a strike on the head. He is now Karuk."

"I heard that story at the Barrow town post office. This Karuk is now famous all right." The men watched the sea ice flash back light to the sun and the water turn deep purple. Suddenly they gave each other playful glances that were signals, put their arms around each other's necks, put their forefingers in the corners of each other's mouths and pulled. They turned their heads with the stretch, laughing and screwing up their faces in pain as they played the old Eskimo game.

[89]

Weir dropped his hand first.

"You win," he said. "We send you to the Eskimo Olympics with Little Owl. She is champion one-foot-high kicker."

"She can reach that little ball on a string one foot above her head and kick it?" Vincent shook his head at the wonder of the little girl running and leaping so high.

Weir did not comment. He was studying the ice, and the water, and the sky.

"Very calm," he said. "But there are no narrow clouds. Are you going to stay?"

"Whale! AġviQ!" Ernie called. His voice was low like a wind. Vincent put aside his gun and sling, as did Weir and Kusiq. Utik awoke. He shook Sagniq and Tigluk. Waldo ran out of the tent. Eyeing each other, not speaking, they grasped the sides of the umiaq and, as one, slid it into the water. Weir climbed aboard and walked to the bow. One by one the others took their seats. Lincoln, who was still standing watch and wondering what was expected of him, saw Vincent beckon to him. He jumped off the perch, stepped into the umiaq and proudly took a seat behind Kusiq. Vincent checked the boat and equipment with an experienced eye, nimbly sat down in the stern, the captain's seat, and pushed off. The crew lifted their paddles and stroked in unison. The whale was about two hundred yards away along the lead edge.

A white blow appeared against the dark water. The whale arched, rose high out of the water and sounded. From a lifetime of whale watching Vincent judged where he would come up. Putting down his paddle and picking up the oar kept in the boat bottom for a rudder, he steered the boat to the precise spot.

Lincoln was gritting his teeth to keep up with the others when Vincent grunted and the paddlers stopped. The umiaq slowed and drifted straight ahead. Vincent leaned on the oar.

With a whoosh a column of spray shot twenty feet into the air not three yards from him. Lincoln instinctively pulled back, then got hold of himself and looked over the gunwale into the huge black blowhole, the nostrils on the top of the whale. Never had he seen such a sight in all his days of whale watching with Uncle Jack on the catboat. He could actually see the water that filled an indentation around the nose holes. An old argument with Uncle Jack was settled. The spray does not come from the lungs, as Uncle Jack believed, or from the mouth, as Lincoln had argued, but from these pockets of water.

As lightly as if he were eiderdown, Weir balanced on the front seat of the boat, his back to the crew. He raised his harpoon above his head. His eyes narrowed as he took aim. Suddenly he nodded and sat down. Weir Amaogak had seen Vincent signal that the hunt was over out of the corner of his eye.

Lincoln was not disappointed. They were right over the whale, and he was enormous. Lincoln could see the huge dark body from beak to flukes as he swam below him in the clear seawater. Lincoln shivered. The head alone was as long as the skin boat. The lower lip, which protruded beyond the upper lip, was white. Enormous fins sculled gracefully under the fragile boat. If the whale merely arched, they would be dumped into the sea, Lincoln feared, goose bumps rising on his spine. But Vincent Ologak knew what he was doing. He held the boat where it was. The whale sucked in air with the force of a giant vacuum and sank without making a ripple. As it swam off, it left its track, and Lincoln saw why Vincent had signaled Weir not to strike. The whale was headed in the wrong direction. It went under the ice. They would have lost it, and there would have been only three whales left for Barrow.

A boat from another camp paddled toward them. They had seen the whale and had come to help. The first crew to strike a bowhead is given credit for it, regardless of who actually kills it or brings it in. Vincent signaled "no whale," and the umiaqs moved apart.

The Ologak crew paddled up and down the lead searching for other bowheads. With the arrival of that whale, the second run was on. A group of beluga whales, actually not whales but dolphins and far smaller than the bowheads, circled the umiaq curiously. Tigluk reached out to touch one, and it grinned at him before sounding. When it came back with three friends, Vincent spoke to them in Iñupiat. They frolicked and flapped their flippers, unafraid of the people. Rarely do the Barrow Eskimo take these little fellows when the bowheads are going by, and the belugas seemed to know it.

"Paddle home," Vincent said after an hour. "No more whales are here."

As the Ologak crew pulled the umiaq up on its ice ramp, Lincoln noticed the seams in the skins he had been kneeling on.

"These seams have needle holes in them," he said, aghast. "They are stitched with needles and threads. Why don't they leak?"

"Special stitching," Weir answered. "Ask Little Owl about it. Annie is teaching her to make skin umiaq covers. She will know how the women hold back the sea."

"Who is Little Owl?"

"My granddaughter." Weir seemed to stretch up an inch taller when he spoke of Little Owl—and he had good reason, as Lincoln would soon find out.

"Come with me," Weir said.

Little Owl was kneeling before a circle of snow blocks stacked in a spiral about three feet high. NatchiQ frolicked around her, sliding in and out between her feet.

"Little Owl," Weir said, "meet Lincoln Noah. Lincoln Noah, meet Ukpik, my little owlet." Lincoln completely forgot the needle holes in the sealskins. Little Owl was beautiful. He was inspired to climb a streetlight and swing down into a cave on ropes.

Out loud he said—and his voice cracked—"You're making a snow house. Wow, I like it. Can you teach me?"

"Bring me one of those snow blocks I've cut and laid over there," she said, a bit peevishly, Lincoln thought. "You can teach yourself."

NatchiQ loped on his belly to greet Lincoln, squeaking like a child running to meet its father at the end of the day. He picked him up and rubbed his chin on the little fellow's sleek head.

"Does the little natchiQ belong to you?" Little Owl snapped.

"I'm his mother, Vincent tells me," Lincoln answered. "I'm feeding him until he is ready to go back to the sea."

"Well, I am building this house for him and me. You are a terrible mother."

Lincoln frowned. "Why do you say that, Little Owl? I love him." He stroked the silvery fur on his back.

"You know why." Her voice trembled.

"No, I don't."

"You tied a coffee can to his flippers. He cried and cried. You're awful. NatchiQ is going to stay with me." Then she drew herself up very straight. "I do not believe a whale is coming to you. It could not. You are cruel."

"Tied a coffee can to him? I didn't!"

"Who did, then? You said you were taking care of him." She shook a snow-cutting knife in Lincoln's face.

He held NatchiQ closer.

"I didn't do it," he said. "But you're right. He should stay in the snow house with you. He needs protection around the clock." He was not off to a good start with Little Owl and did not know what to do about it. He could not tell her who had tied the can on NatchiQ's tail, although he certainly knew.

Lincoln watched Little Owl cut blocks out of patches of the hard, wind-driven snow. He carried them to the snow house and, hopeful that he could repair the damage done to him, held them in place while she trimmed and shaped them to smoothness. After they had laid several more spirals of blocks, the house was a dome.

"Nifty," Lincoln said, stepping back to inspect the graceful shelter.

"We need a clear piece of ice for the top," Little Owl said. "So I can see who's coming." She flashed him a meaningful glance, and once more he did not know what to say.

By the time he returned from the lead edge with a clear piece of ice, Little Owl had made a qanitchaq and was crawling down the tunnel-like arch into her iglu.

"Bring NatchiQ in," she called. "But be kind to him." Stuffing NatchiQ inside his parka, Lincoln went into the glowing house on hands and knees.

"This is wonderful," he said, looking around. "So silent and beautiful. So very silent. I can hardly hear my own voice." He glanced at Little Owl. Her face was knotted with anger.

"You must believe me," he said. "I did not tie the tin

can to NatchiQ's feet." Little Owl studied the tips of her boots, then looked up. Her brown eyes bored into him.

"All right," she answered. "But I will take him with me to eat." She gathered him up and crawled down the qanitchaq, leaving Lincoln alone.

"Like Romeo," he said to himself, "I've got everything going against me." He slid out of the snow house and walked to the edge of the ice to console himself by watching the seals play.

When those who were not sleeping finished today's menu of walrus stew and a batch of Eskimo doughnuts Bertha had made to celebrate Weir's arrival, Vincent took his old friend's arm and they walked to the edge of the ice. Vincent dropped a feather onto the water.

"The current has changed," he said.

"Not good. It flows south."

Vincent threw a handful of snow into the air. "No wind."

"Strange combination," said Weir.

Lincoln did not understand what they had said, for they were talking in melodious Iñupiat. Weary and hungry, he walked into the tent. Tigluk sat in the furs shuffling the pinochle deck. Little Owl was not around. He strode up to Tigluk, his fists clenched.

"Tigluk?"

The young man did not look up.

"Ologak Camp," the CB sputtered. "This is Ologak Base in Barrow. Do you copy. Over?"

"I copy you. Over," Bertha answered.

"This is your office, Bertha. There's a young person

here who needs to talk to you. He has some cocaine somewhere. He is having trouble with it. He needs your counsel. Over."

"How did he get it?"

"Someone on the afternoon plane."

"How I hate the planes," Bertha said. "They bring in liquor and drugs—and ruin us. I cannot come in, Sarah. Send him out. Tell him to go through the whalebone arch and follow the ice trail that goes north. Over."

"See any whales, Bertha?"

"One. It was too near the ice. What do the other camps see? Over."

"They are all closed in except you and the Kakinya crew, who are also on your lead. Rudd's crew was west of you. They moved an hour ago. The ice hit. Over."

"All right; we'll watch. Who is the boy you are sending? Over."

"Roy."

She looked at the dwindling supplies and the already-cramped tent.

"Cocaine?" she said sorrowfully. "Over."

"Cocaine. Over."

"Send him out." She flipped the switch.

Lincoln was distressed: drugs, alcohol, restrictions on whaling—no wonder the Eskimos hated outsiders. He picked up a doughnut and sat down near Bertha, his wrath for Tigluk gone.

"Are you a counsellor, Bertha?" he asked, for it had never occurred to him that she might have another job.

She was Vincent Ologak's wife and the whale-camp manager.

"I am a member of the Circumpolar Health Council." She shook her head. "We have lots of problems all right. The clash of the old and the new and too much money. Lots of our young people are all mixed up." Tigluk shuffled the cards.

After a long silence Lincoln crawled into his sleeping bag, picked up Waldo's copy of *The Tundra Times* and read himself to sleep.

Around midnight Weir came into the tent and tapped Vincent, who had closed his eyes but was not sleeping.

"Sagvaq, the current," he said. "It is rushing north like a snow machine."

Vincent got to his feet and put on his parka and snow shirt.

"Call the weather station, Bertha," he said, shaking her awake. "See what is happening." He followed Weir outside.

The sticks Utik had put down were almost eighty feet apart, and the crack was two feet wide.

"Off the ice!" Vincent called. "Sagniq, Tigluk; come off watch! The ice is going out!" He glanced at the midnight sun. Narrow clouds were strung across it like red threads.

"Off the ice!"

"Get up, Lincoln," Bertha called. "Close the stoves. Pack the pots and pans in the food box. Put them on a sled." She ran to the snow house.

"Little Owl. Off the ice. We go."

As Lincoln carried the food box outside, Kusiq drove up with the last of the four snow machines, jumped off and began hitching them to Vincent's sleds. Little Owl and Weir had packed their sled, and Waldo and Ernie were lashing the umiaq to another. The ice was moaning and throbbing under their feet. The chunk where the boat had sat broke off and swirled out into the steely water. Ernie loaded the kerosene heating stove, and Bertha stowed the CB beside it. The tent was empty. Tigluk and Vincent knocked the steel tent stakes out of the ice with hammers. Lincoln picked up a hammer and hit a spike. The ice shattered around it, then split open like a log. Water gurgled below his feet.

The crack widened. The tent fell. Sagniq dropped onto it and rolled it up even while it was still fluttering down. Vincent pulled it onto a sled.

Only the plywood floor remained to say where the Ologak whale camp had been. Kusiq grabbed one end of a stack of four plywood sheets, Waldo the other. They tossed them onto the last sled and piled the sleeping skins and whale knives on top. Now there was nothing left but the sea ice and the water's fingers that were creeping up through the cracks.

Weir signaled Little Owl to get on the snow machine behind him, started the engine and pulled out. Tigluk jumped onto a machine, jumped off and ran to another. He mumbled to Vincent, who was standing on the rear of a sled, "I'll let Lincoln have the new one. He loves snow machines."

In fifteen minutes the camp that had been Lincoln's

home for almost four days was gone and three of Vincent's four snow machines were roaring and ready to go.

"Lincoln Noah," Vincent called. "Drive the orange machine! Everyone follow Kusiq.

"Kusiq, drive against the current. Look for a bridge. We are adrift." They took off.

Lincoln pulled the starter cord. The engine would not start. He pulled again. Nothing. Again. Again. The other three machines and Weir were moving swiftly away.

"I'm panicking," he said to himself when the machine would not start on the fifth pull. "Take it easy, Lincoln. Take it easy." He raised the hood, found the spark plug wires had been disconnected, put them back and, taking a deep breath, placed his fingers around the cord grip again. He pulled hard and evenly. It started. Lincoln jumped on the seat and turned the handles to feed gas to the sputtering engine. The machine moved forward.

Kusiq was three hundred feet ahead, shooting swiftly toward the pivot point of the moving floe. Lincoln concentrated on reaching him, and with torturous slowness began to close the distance.

"NatchiQ!" He stopped the snow machine and looked back. An enormous slab of blue ice was rising over the snow house. The monolith reared up, hung motionless for a moment, then crashed with a thundering explosion. The little house tipped and turned over.

"NatchiQ, forgive me." He pressed his lips together, accelerated and sped after his crew. They were crossing the ice bridge to safety far ahead of him.

Keeping in their tracks, he drove up to the top of an ice pile. There he stopped short and turned off the motor. Two feet of water separated him from the land-side bulk of the floating ice, and it was rapidly becoming three.

His friends stared helplessly at him; then Weir, who had unpacked a rope, hurled it across the water.

It fell at Lincoln's feet. He grabbed it, looped it around the machine and, turning on all the power, drove down the ice, bounced, and shot through the air and across the water. He hit the other side with the treads. They spun, dug in and pulled him to safety.

The front of the sled was across, but the rear was in the water, sinking. Lincoln gunned the engine. The track slipped on the ice, and the heavy sled began pulling Lincoln and the machine down toward the sea. But he did not get off. He had to save Vincent's sled and machine. Carefully, he fed the gas.

"Pull! Pull!" Lincoln looked up. Kusiq, Utik, Weir, Sagniq, Waldo, Ernie, Bertha and Little Owl were hauling on the rope. Tigluk was tinkering with a sled.

"Pull! Pull!" Vincent called out. The machine crept forward; then a block of ice hit the sled and knocked it at right angles to the machine. It would not track when it was at that angle. Lincoln gunned the engine and skidded the machine, as Uncle Jack used to do when he rounded corners in his car in ski country. The machine lined up with the sled.

"Pull!" The crew pulled. Lincoln slowly turned up the gas.

"Pull!" The sled came out of the water and up onto the ice. Everyone cheered.

In the gold light of one A.M. Vincent Ologak's whaling crew were resting on the land-fast ice. Bertha had gotten out the Coleman stove and coffeepot and was making hot coffee. As the brew slipped down the weary whalers, they recovered their strength and began to sing. Lincoln listened and watched the red-orange sun climb the sky. The twilight of night was over. Another day had begun even while the last seemed not to have ended.

When Vincent and Weir had finished their coffee, they climbed a pressure ridge to get a wide view of the sea ice. Their lead was freckled with floes moving south, and the narrow clouds were gone. In their place was a mass of white-and-blue clouds billowing over the pack ice.

"Now anugI comes." Vincent pointed to the wind cloud. "We must move again." The two elders walked back to the crew.

"AnugI," Vincent announced. "We drive to that distant glacier and get behind it."

Lincoln led the caravan this time.

The Ologak crew had hardly pulled up behind the forty-foot-high rock of ice before the anugI wind struck with the force of a hurricane. Safe from its blast, the whalers hunched on the lee side of their sleds, their knees pulled up to their chins, their heads down. The glacier took the punishment. The anugI carved deep scallops on its windward side.

Lincoln listened to the wind. It sounded like trains roaring downhill, jets taking off, avalanches crashing down mountains. He blew his breath into his wolverine trim and thought about Uncle Jack.

"I hope you went to Florida," he said.

"Lincoln?" It was Little Owl. She had crept through the blowing snow and wind to find him. "NatchiQ will be all right," she said. "He will fall into the sea and call. The other seals will find him and adopt him as you did."

"Thank you," he said. "I am worried about him. He trusted me." Lincoln put his head on his knees, and his eyes closed from exhaustion.

"Lincoln?" Little Owl's voice sounded warm and friendly.

"What?"

"I know who tied the coffee can on NatchiQ's feet. Forgive me."

"I forgave you the moment I saw you."

Little Owl blushed and smiled. "Lincoln?"

"What?"

"Want to learn how to do the one-foot-high kick?"

"Sure. What is it?"

"You kick a ball on a string one foot above your head. You are nimble. You could win. There's a contest at the Blanket Toss Festival."

"What's the Blanket Toss Festival?"

"The whale festival, Nalukataq. Vincent Ologak's crew will set the date."

"Why will we set it?"

"The captain who gets the first whale sets the date. We are going to get the first whale." Lincoln lifted his head. With Little Owl beside him his weariness was gone. He longed to hold her hand and thank her for comforting him, but he was too stiff and cold to move.

"The festival is a lot of fun," she went on. "People come from all the villages. Everyone is invited. Lots of maktak, lots of goose, Eskimo doughnuts, walrus, seal, caribou—and then there's the blanket toss. We are tossed high in the air on a trampoline of skins. We fly like a bird and come back down. The blanket toss is really fun."

"Maybe I can't do a one-foot-high kick," Lincoln said. "Then what?"

"You could do a one-arm reach. All you have to do is stand on one hand, reach up with the other and hit a ball that is on a string above your head.

"Or you could throw the whale lance like Kusiq does. He is very good at that. He wins every time." Lincoln did not take up the subject. She thought harder.

"You could do the seal walk."

"What's that?"

"Walk on your hands with your legs off the ground, parallel to the floor."

"You're kidding!"

"No, I'm not. Kusiq will show you. You can do it, because . . ." AnugI, the wind, took her words and flung them far over the sea ice and he did not hear, "because Lincoln Noah, I have changed my mind about you. I believe a whale is coming to you."

SEVEN

Siku, the pack ice

THERE WERE no watches at Vincent Ologak's second whale camp. The wind that blew for a day came out of the southwest and closed the last leads between Wainwright and Barrow. Only part of the whale puddle remained open.

The tent was set up behind the ship-shaped glacier, but the umiaq remained on its sled, waiting for the north wind to open the leads and let the whalers chase the whales who were now locked off from them, swimming under the ice.

A pinochle game was in progress inside the warm tent. Little Owl offered Lincoln a cup of coffee, then sat down beside him. Ever since the incident with the tampered snow machine, Little Owl had been looking at him with shy smiles and talking pleasantly with him. Nothing could have pleased Lincoln more.

Bertha flipped on the CB and called her office.

"Roy turned back when the storm hit," a woman said. "Over."

"Send him right out here. Before it's too late. Over."

Vincent put down his cards and looked at Bertha. "I do not like it," he said. "I do not like Roy here. This is whale camp."

"We must save our young people," Bertha snapped. "What better place than whale camp, where tradition is strong?"

"We must have young people who are quick in whale camp," Vincent replied angrily. "Not drugged ones."

"He needs you," Bertha said, raising her voice. "Help him."

"Ah," said Vincent, shaking his head. "We argue. We need a whale to bind us. We need the spirit of the whale in our hearts, Bertha."

"We need the spirit of the whale in our hearts," she said. "Let Roy come."

"I think," said Utik in a booming voice, "that it is time I catch some big fresh tom cods and some crabs so we have something nice to celebrate." He picked up a fishing line and a long-handled ice cutter and went out of the tent. Little Owl busied herself sweeping the plywood floor.

"Lincoln Noah," said Kusiq, also eager to leave the uncomfortable scene between Bertha and Vincent, "come outside. I show you how to do the seal for Nalukataq." Lincoln gladly followed.

Out on the ice Utik was standing patiently over a hole not far from the glacier.

"Come, aġviQ," he sang in Iñupiat. "Come, great Nukik.

Bring peace to us." Little Owl heard and wished for a whale to happen to them.

The pinochle game, which had stopped while the Ologaks argued, resumed without Vincent. Waldo took his place, but the game quickly broke up. Tigluk cheated and Waldo ran him outside. Laughing uproariously, Tigluk sat down on a sled and took out his bone carving. His father put down a whale knife he was sharpening and walked over to him.

"Tigluk, you are no good. Why do I have a son like you?"

Tigluk hunkered down and said nothing.

"Your brother Frank is not like this. He studies and works hard. He wins honors. He makes me proud. You make only trouble for me."

Tigluk had heard this so many times, he simply clenched his jaws together and tightened his parka hood so he could not hear. He stared resentfully at Kusiq and Lincoln, two "good" boys like his brother, and wished he had a six-pack of beer.

"Your hands are too far forward," Kusiq said to Lincoln, who shifted them. "Good; now keep your legs straight, lift and walk." With great effort, Lincoln inched his legs and toes off the ice, wobbled and fell back.

"You got the idea," said Kusiq. "Now practice. The one who stays up the longest and walks the farthest wins. Time me." He took off his wristwatch and handed it to Lincoln. It was a jogger's digital watch.

"This looks like an invader from another planet," Lincoln chided. "Does it have a restaurant on it? It's got everything else."

Kusiq laughed and got down on his belly. He placed his fists under his hips, arranged and rearranged them, then pressed and lifted his legs. "Count."

Even with his boots on, he raised his feet high off the ice and, waddling from side to side like a seal, began to walk. He did indeed look like NatchiQ, the seal.

"Twenty-eight seconds, twenty-nine seconds."

Kusiq grunted and came down to measure his distance.

"Twenty-nine seconds. Wow. Strong boy all right," Lincoln said.

Kusiq rolled onto his back and smiled at Lincoln's words.

"You Eskimo all right," he said. Lincoln was surprised how good those words made him feel. There was something secure and strong in the Eskimo personality, and the longer he lived with them, the more he wished to be one, not just in blood but in deeds and spirit.

"Your turn to do the seal," Kusiq said.

Lincoln was just about to lift his feet when Little Owl stepped out of the tent and tossed out the dishwater. It went up in the subzero air as hot water and hit the ground as ice. Lincoln stared at the crystal balls bouncing toward him.

"Diamonds for you, Lincoln Noah," she called happily, and came over to watch the workout.

"I forget how cold it is out here in my warm clothes," Lincoln said. "Until you all do something like that." He rearranged his hands.

"Little Owl"—he looked up at her—"can you do the seal?"

"Last year I could," she said as she scrubbed the pan with snow. "This year I cannot." She patted her hips. "I have changed into a woman. My weight is in the wrong place."

Lincoln thought that was very nice and stared happily at the pale-blue ice under his nose. Taking off a mitten, he thoughtfully stroked the fuzz on his upper lip, wondering if the time had come for him to shave.

"What are you stalling for?" Kusiq asked. He knew perfectly well that Little Owl was the reason and felt a twinge of jealousy. Until this moment Lincoln had been the almost holy boy to whom the whale was coming. But Kusiq decided here and now he did not have to like everything about him. "I am going to practice my lance throw if you do not stop stalling around," he snapped. "I have better things to do."

"Stalling?" Lincoln said. "Me stalling? Guess I am." With warm thoughts of Little Owl powering his arms and legs, he lifted his feet. Four seconds later he thumped back onto the ice. He lifted them again, felt his muscles strain; then his legs, body, face and crooked nose collapsed onto the ice. He breathed ice crystals. But he had not done badly.

"Hey," he said to himself. "With Little Owl for inspiration, I just might get good enough to enter the seal-walk contest at the whale festival—what is it called—Nalukataq."

Vincent came out of the tent frowning and looking

miserable. He did not want Roy in camp, but he also did not want to fight with Bertha. Quietly he checked the sleds and the tent ropes. He retied a paddle in the ice-bound umiaq, and after blowing his nose, he wiped his eyes.

When he could find nothing else to do, he climbed the pale-green iceberg until he could see far across the sea of ice, which seemed to be personally challenging the Ologak crew and testing their strength.

A change came over Vincent Ologak as he studied the top of the world. His eyes brightened and color rushed into his face. The great white habitat of the whales and seals, of the polar bears and walruses, of the gulls and terns, of the eider ducks and of the Eskimos, glared at him. The needs of his people stirred his deepest feelings. Two years without a whale had brought a great unhappiness to the people of Barrow and himself. He must get a whale.

"Nukik?" he whispered. "I feel you out there. The boy is here. The time has come."

All Vincent's senses tuned in on the whale, and he became an instrument to which nature spoke. Listening to the wind, the air pressure, the ice, the water, the sky, he hunched down in his parka, a small owllike figure on the cold green top of the gigantic iceberg. Kusiq and Little Owl were watching from below. They could not take their eyes from him. Utik put down his fishing line, Ernie and Sagniq stopped scraping the polar-bear skin and Tigluk looked up. The scowls on his face unraveled. Lincoln, still on his belly and facedown, heard the silence. He rolled over and, as if Vincent had called to him, looked up.

The whaling captain felt the atmospheric pressure and the humidity; he observed the fog and the sun dogs, a trick of the frozen mist that makes the sun two glowing suns in the sky. He listened to the ice speak about the wind and current, and the wind and current speak about the whales. After a long while he came down the wind-carved glacier, picking his way with precision.

"Nukik," he said to his attentive whalers, "is still in the whale puddle where Weir saw him. The ice says, 'No change.' We wait.

"Lincoln Noah, get the orange snow machine and the sled. We are going on a drive."

Lincoln picked himself up and promptly hitched a sled to the snow machine, which was in camp. They were not whaling, and silence was not a concern. Bertha piled the sled with furs, and Vincent Ologak climbed aboard.

"Are you going to Barrow town?" Waldo asked the whaling captain. "My office needs me. My boss told Bertha the printer broke down."

"I can drop you off," Vincent said. Waldo climbed aboard, and Vincent bobbed his head asking Weir to come, too. The harpooner stepped on the back footboard and held on. A few strands of grizzly hair showed under the beaver-skin hat that he wore under his parka hood in the coldest weather. The slits in his wooden sunglasses shone black, and Weir Amaogak looked as if he had come from the wolves when the world turned over.

No one else asked to come along. They had heard

Vincent's silent language of the ice, and the message was "That's all." Lincoln had become very aware of this communications system when they were hunting the whale in the umiaq, but as yet he did not understand more than a few simple eye signals. However, when he looked back at Vincent for instructions, he suddenly knew that the elder's eyes were clearly saying, "Let's go." In awe of the incredible silence that talked, he pulled the starter cord and drove off.

He was still puzzling over this language when the electric poles of Barrow came into view. He glanced back. Vincent's eyes did not speak. He drove on.

Shortly, they came to a crossroads of orange and green trail markers, and Lincoln stopped for directions. Waldo got off the sled, waved good-bye, and started off on the short trek to Barrow on foot. Lincoln was wondering what to do next when Vincent's silent message came through.

"Follow the orange flags," said his eyes and head movements. Lincoln instinctively answered "Okay" with eye contact, and he felt he was on page one of a first-grade reader.

The orange-flagged trail snaked around huge ice blocks, across open flats and along the edge of the shore to finally arrive at a radio tower. Vincent signaled, "Stop."

"End of the United States, Point Barrow," said Weir, walking up to Lincoln. The wind-packed snow smoothed the landscape so that Lincoln could not tell where the U.S. ended and the ocean began. Searching for some difference, he turned slowly and looked out upon a cluster of enormous whale jawbones standing like gaunt giants on the bleak tundra. They leaned toward the north, pointing to the wind that opens the leads.

"The graves of ancient whaling captains," Vincent said. "Once there was an Eskimo village here, so long ago even the elders do not remember it." He squinted, as if to see into the past and discover where he had come from and who he was.

"It is said," he went on, "that this land was once connected to Siberia. That is what our elders teach us—that we came from there hundreds of generations ago."

"The people who lived here"—Weir spoke in muted tones—"may have been the spirits-who-came-around-the-bend that my elders talk about. The people-who-came-around-the-bend lived so far back in time, no one re-

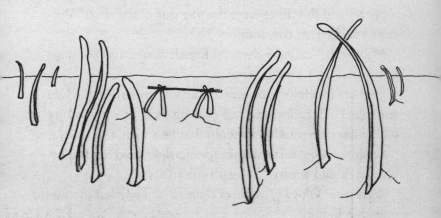

members. Maybe the bend they rounded was the land bridge between Alaska and Siberia. I do not know. But I do know these ancient bones mark the graves of whaling captains as they do today. The spirits here were whaling captains."

Weir and Vincent lapsed into Iñupiat, not to exclude Lincoln but to talk about a time and happenings for which there were no English words.

"Follow the orange markers," Vincent said in English.

Half an hour later Lincoln spotted what seemed to be a wooden matchbox on the sea of ice. As he approached, it grew to be a large packing crate, once used to ship a truck or snow machine to the Arctic. The white men in the Arctic had learned ingenuity and full use of materials from the Eskimos. The shed bristled with as many antennae as a porcupine has quills.

"Science camp," he said to himself. "Hot diggity."

When he had turned off the noisy engine, he heard whistles and flutelike songs floating out of the shed. Vincent knocked on the door.

"Come in," called a cheerful female voice, and the door flew open on a young woman.

Barbara Morley's sunburned nose was coated with white sun block. A round spot of peeling skin from frostbite on her cheek reminded Lincoln that he was in the Arctic. The bite was not unattractive, for it emphasized her bright-blue eyes and pretty V-shaped mouth.

"Vincent Ologak," she exclaimed. "To what do we owe this honor?"

"Hey, Vincent," called a man from the dark rear of the shed. "It's me, Chuck Riley. We met at the mayor's office last month." Professor Riley from M.I.T. was a newcomer to science camp. An acoustics expert, he had been hired to count whales by their voices, which could be heard as far as ten miles away on underwater hydrophones even when the leads were closed. The people who tallied the whales by sight could not count when the fog or pack ice closed in, and many whales were not recorded.

Chuck was listening to the whistles and trills and adjusting dials on a bank of electronic equipment. The Ologak crew squeezed into the small hut and closed out the bitter cold.

Vincent stepped forward and cocked his ear to a speaker, the better to hear the sounds of the sea mammals calling under the ice. Their voices were being picked up by three hydrophones and radioed to the shack, where they were taped, printed on sonograph paper and mapped.

"No whales," Vincent said.

"None for two days," Chuck replied. "You see any?"

"All the leads are closed. Very bad ice conditions."

"Something has happened," Barbara said. "The migration has stopped."

"That is correct," Vincent said. "The hydrophones tell you that?" He seemed pleased. "The ice tells me the current has changed, and pretty soon we shall see whales."

"You're a lot more sensitive than our equipment," Chuck said. "Our hydrophones can tell us only that there are no whales making sounds. They could be going by in silence, as they regularly do, but our gear cannot say so."

Vincent listened to the seals. They seemed very active. He turned to Weir and spoke in Iñupiat.

"Nukik, you say, is with his granddaughter?"

Weir nodded.

"It is good," Vincent said.

"It is good," Weir agreed in his own tongue. "Or he would have gone under the ice with his pod and passed us by. He would have been too far out to find the boy."

A low sigh sounded above the trill of the seals, and Vincent took off the beaver hat that he, like Weir, wore under his parka hood on cold days and listened intently.

"Pack ice," he said. "Very heavy ice."

"Pack ice?" asked Chuck Riley. "Is it coming our way?" Science camp was also forced to move frequently.

Vincent did not answer immediately; he was listening to another sound coming over the system. His eyes brightened. He held up his hand.

"Thump, thump, thump. Hear it? Polar bear. Polar bear walking on the ice. Good instrument to pick up a polar bear."

"Good man to know it's a bear," said Barbara, and flipped on the two-way radio.

"Castle Perch, this is Acoustics. Do you copy?"

"I copy you, Acoustics." The radio sputtered and crackled so much that the voice on the other end sounded more mechanical than human.

"We are hearing a polar bear. I repeat, we are hearing a polar bear at hydrophone two. He is near you. Be on the lookout."

"Roger, I hear you. A polar bear is near. Thank you, Acoustics. Fog has rolled in. We cannot see far. Over."

"That's Musk Ox," Barbara said to Lincoln. "He's about half a mile out at one of the two perches where the watchers count whales by sight. We count by sound, and together we get some idea of how many there are. I hope Musk Ox doesn't go looking for that bear in the fog. He just might. He's that kind of guy." The tramping of the bear became louder, then began to fade.

"He's going away—out onto the pack ice," Vincent said, and Chuck and Barbara relaxed and turned down the sound.

"How did a man get a name like Musk Ox?" Lincoln asked when the trouble seemed to be over.

"Musk oxen are wild cows of the Arctic, big wooly creatures with heads of curled horns," Barbara explained. "They take on enemies by gathering in a circle and facing them. We call this tanik Musk Ox because he faces his enemies and fights head-on."

"Enemies? Who are his enemies?"

"People who don't want the Eskimos to whale."

"Oh," Lincoln said . . . and knew that Musk Ox could not be Uncle Jack. He was about to ask Barbara if she knew Jack James, but Chuck turned up the volume to let Vincent hear a beluga whale, and he decided to come back and ask later.

The beluga warbled; the seals sang like birds, chirping and trilling as they talked about their territories and their blue-green dens under the ice. They also sang out to say who they were and where they were hunting. Suddenly, as if all the sea mammals were tired of hearing each other, they stopped burbling.

"How many whales have you counted this season?" Vincent asked Chuck in the silence.

"In four days we heard over four thousand bowhead vocalizations. Musk Ox and his crew, who count by sight, saw fifty we did not hear. Putting that all through the computer, we come up with two hundred whales passing Barrow in four days."

"Lotsa maktak," Weir said.

"Lot more whales than we thought," Barbara agreed. "Looks like the Eskimo are right. There are quite a few bowheads in the sea."

Vincent Ologak smiled with satisfaction. It was he who had made the arrangements, egged on by Annie's love of education, for the university-trained scientists to count the bowheads. Although he and Weir and other whalers knew there were many more than one or two thousand bowheads in their sea, Vincent had wanted the white man to know it, too.

Suddenly he bent closer to the receiver and put his hands behind his ears to capture the sound.

"I hear siku," he said. "The pack ice."

Chuck cocked his ear.

"The low roar?"

"The low roar. Same over the hydrophones as out on the ice. And it says, 'I am moving.' Siku is holding back the second run of whales. There are thousands in that run. The bowhead is returning—just in time to save the Eskimo."

"Thousands in the second run?" Barbara asked.

"Thousands," Vincent repeated. "I know this not through hydrophones, but through my long life."

"I wouldn't have believed you last year," Barbara said. "But after Chuck installed the hydrophones this year, we're tracking many whales we cannot see. We're beginning to find out what you have known all along. The whales have made a nice comeback—not great, but nice."

"Survival makes the Eskimo the scientists of the north all right. We have to know these things to stay alive." Vincent's eyes twinkled. Chuck grinned and peered out of the small window at the billowing fog that was now moving in from Castle Perch.

"You think the pack ice is moving in, Vincent?" He sincerely respected the Eskimo's knowledge when it came to interpreting the ice.

"You have about six hours before you have to move," Vincent replied. Suddenly he clutched Lincoln's arm to steady himself.

"Too hot in here. Take me out." It was not the heat, Lincoln knew, as he and Weir helped Vincent out the door and through the fog that had rolled in from Castle Perch. The whaling captain's breath was coming in great gasps.

Lincoln pulled the starter cord, and in his nervousness the engine spluttered and died. In the quiet he heard voices through the thin plywood walls of the shed:

"Acoustics, this is Castle Perch. Musk Ox speaking. Do you copy?" The voice was still metallic with static.

"I copy you, Musk Ox. Go ahead."

"Thanks for the bear info. It was forty feet from the cook tent. A rifle blast turned it away. Dangerous situation. Thanks again. Over."

"Roger. Thank Vincent Ologak. He heard it on the hydrophones."

"Vincent Ologak? Is he there? Over."

"He was. Know him? Over."

"I know him well. I know him very well. He and I did battle once. Over."

"Well, listen to this, bonny camp director. Vincent Ologak said siku, the pack ice, will hit in six hours. Over."

"Siku anayanaqtuq—anayanaqtuq."

"What? Over."

"Get off the ice. Pack up. We're moving now. Over."

"Roger. Pack up now."

At the crossroads Lincoln stopped to get his bearings and check on Vincent Ologak.

"I feel pretty good," Vincent said. "Better than I have in days." And as if to prove it, he put his boots down and walked to Weir, who was up on an ice mound studying the horizon, which was fogless here.

"Siku," Vincent said, pointing. The horizon was mov-

[120]

ing. Building-sized ice blocks were tumbling like corn flakes as the pack ice bulldozed toward land. Not far away a vast arena of flat ice snapped, rose into a teepee and crumbled into ice corn. The sound thundered in.

Lincoln looked down at his feet, shuddering to realize he was standing on ice that the summer sun was returning to water. Barrow town was only a dash away. He shot it a worried glance and definitely felt like running there with all speed.

"Water sky!" Weir lifted both hands toward a thin black cloud rising this side of the buckling horizon.

"We go to it," Vincent said.

"We go?" Weir asked. "While the pack ice is moving?"

"Siku is already moving out. A strong current has reversed its flow. Soon we will feel the change here. The ice will stop crumbling before we get to camp."

Vincent put a hand on Weir's shoulder. "Nukik is coming, my beloved friend."

As they sped back to camp, cracks that had not been there on the trip out festooned the trail like jagged ribbons. At each one Lincoln checked Vincent's reaction. Apparently he had nothing to say but "Go to the water sky."

They rode up to the tent and stopped.

"Off the ice," Vincent ordered. No one argued or asked why. Boxes were slammed closed and stowed. The tent fluttered down. Skins were loaded, snow machines started.

"To the water sky." Vincent climbed onto Weir's sled and sat down beside Bertha. He took her hand. "A whale is coming," he said, and they smiled at each other and knew it was so.

"To the water sky!" Little Owl saw that Vincent and Bertha had taken her spot on Weir's sled and, waving to her Ataata to say she would not ride with him, jumped onto the seat behind Lincoln. He started off with a jerk and she grabbed him around the waist.

"I'll bet I can stay up twenty-two seconds and hit a bull's-eye with a lance," he thought as her arms tightened around him. Inspired, he drove up an ice hill, shot off into the air, thumped to the ground and rushed toward the water sky. A mile along, Weir stopped the caravan to chop a passage through an enormous pressure ridge. Lincoln and Little Owl parked and ran ahead to help.

They were walking back to their sled when a cloud of fog came over the ridge and poured down the ice like thick cream. Lincoln could see nothing.

"Crawl on your hands and knees," Little Owl said. "You can see the snow machine tread marks in the ice if you get your face close enough."

When they finally found their rig, the others had driven off in the fog.

"I'm going to wait until this clears," Lincoln said, feeling blindly for the driving handles.

"Go!" Little Owl urged. "This is nothing. If we stay here, we are lost."

He inched the machine through the pass, stopped, heard the crew ahead and crept on. At the bottom of another ridge the fog thinned and he drove up it—into sunshine. The Ologak crew was nowhere to be seen, but the great black cloud hung just ahead.

"Follow the water sky," Ukpik said without even a tremor in her voice. Lincoln eased the machine and sled down the murky ridge.

"Go right. Take that little valley; go left. Up to the right."

"What's that!" Lincoln pulled up to a dark object in a drift.

A snowmobile lay upside down in the bank. Beside it a fur-clad figure was clawing with bare hands at the ice.

"It's Roy," said Little Owl. Lincoln dropped to his knees beside him. "Be careful. He looks all druggy. He is mean on drugs."

Lincoln managed to turn him onto his back. Roy stared up at him through misty, unseeing eyes.

"He's badly wasted," Little Owl said. Suddenly she glanced at her feet. "The ice is moving. Lincoln. Go! We cannot help him, or we die, too."

Although siku had crashed into the shore-fast ice a mile from Lincoln and Little Owl, the tremor was only now reaching the spot where they stood. The shock waves from the collision were powerful and loud. Lincoln thought he had been thrown off the earth and was riding the solar winds. He ran for the machine, heeding Little Owl, then turned back to Roy.

Little Owl started the snow machine.

"Get on, Lincoln!" An avalanche of ice blocks was rolling toward them, relentless and unstoppable. Ice chunks bounced up in front of it like Ping-Pong balls. On and on and on it came, and no human hands or machines could halt it.

Lincoln grabbed Roy under the armpits and pulled him to his knees.

"Whahaha ya want."

"Get on the sled," Lincoln ordered. The white-man accent was like a knife in Roy's face. He stumbled to his feet.

"Tanik!" he sneered. "Gea off the ish. Hea me?" He took a wide stance and grabbed Lincoln's throat.

"White man. I keel you all right." Roy's brain seemed to clear when he clutched Lincoln's throat.

"You take our hunting land. You take our whales. You take our animals. You slowly kill my people. I kill you fast."

The fingers tightened. Lincoln tore at their wild strength but could not release them. With a loud grunt he pounded a fist into Roy's ear. Roy let go. Lincoln dropped to his knees and dove for Roy's legs. He brought him down onto the ice with a thud.

Infuriated, Roy pulled his knife.

"I'll shoot!" Little Owl held her gun in Roy's face.

Seeing her with Lincoln enraged Roy even more. "Get away from her. She is ours." As he reached for his gun, Lincoln struck him under the chin with all his strength, and like the great white polar bear, Roy crumpled to the ground.

"Thank heavens," said Little Owl. "He's out." She put her gun back in the carrying case.

"Grab his feet," Lincoln said. "I'll take his shoulders. We'll throw him on the sled."

"And tie him there," she added. Lincoln worked fast. The ice avalanche had rolled over Roy's snow machine and was spreading toward them like a river delta. But it had spent its jolt from the pack ice, and it slowed down and stopped short of the orange snow machine. As Vincent had said at the crossroads, the pack ice had changed its course. It was going out. The change reached the ridge where Little Owl and Lincoln were tying Roy on the sled, and it reached them not one minute too soon.

"Follow the water sky," Little Owl said, and climbing on the backseat of the snow machine, she put her arms snugly around Lincoln.

EIGHT

Aquun, the rudder

LITTLE OWL pointed the way to the water sky, skimming them over skating rinks and around ice boulders until Lincoln was so confused, he pulled up to a pressure ridge and stopped. Together they climbed the sparkling hill, Little Owl picking their way.

"The lead!" she exclaimed when she reached the top. "Hallelujah, hallelujah. A whale is coming to you."

Lincoln scrambled the last few feet on hands and knees. The black water sky they had been chasing was a cloud hanging low over a meandering river of marine-blue seawater. In it seals cavorted and little beluga whales caught shrimp and fish.

"Everything's going to be all right," Little Owl said. "Nukik is coming. We will dance and beat the drums. We will love each other again." She pulled her wolverine ruff around her face, for the wind was strong on the top of the pressure ridge.

"Do you see our crew?" Lincoln asked. Little Owl scanned the green-blue and white icescape.

"There!" She pointed to a small line of antlike objects on a vast crystal flat. It was creeping toward the cloud-hung lead. "No, wait a minute," she corrected herself. "I think that's Rudd's crew. He has all green snow machines." Lincoln handed her the binoculars he was still wearing, and she focused the eyepieces.

"That's Rudd all right," she said. "He's a trouble-maker. He's one of the radical Eskimos."

"A radical Eskimo?"

"He fights the taniks' and the government's hunting and fishing rules, particularly the quota on whales. He brags that he will go over our limit no matter how much he is fined."

"How much are the fines?"

"Ten thousand dollars." She focused the binoculars more finely on the line of green ants.

"Looks like the Rudds will be our neighbors," she said. "They are headed for the same open water." She gave the binoculars back to Lincoln. "I'm sorry for that. Otis Rudd does not like Vincent. Whaling requires good feel-ing—lots of cooperation." Little Owl looked down at Roy in the sled below them. He was quite still. She took off her mittens and looped them behind her back on their long string, then sat down on a block of ice.

"Whaling is the most important thing we do as Eski-mos," she said. "We return to the old ways and old values when we whale. We find our roots. We care about each other again. Caring has kept us alive in the Arctic for thousands of years. You can't whale with someone you don't love."

Lincoln liked what she was saying. He sat down beside the little fur-clad girl, who sat, back straight, atop a block of ice in the forbidding wilderness.

"You know so much," he said.

"I don't know nearly enough. I'm going to college when I grow up. Then I'm going to get a master's degree, and then a Ph.D.—from Harvard."

"A Ph.D. from Harvard? That will take you far away from Barrow."

Little Owl pushed back her ruff to make certain the next words were not muddled.

"I'll learn—it is very important that I learn what the taniks know. I am now learning the great knowledge of our elders. I listen and write down all they do and say—how to sew, how to spear seal, how to whale, where we came from, all of it. When I know as much as I can about my people, then I will go to Harvard. I will learn as much as I can from the taniks.

"I will come back to my people and help to save them from extinction. We will not exist if we lose our ways and culture—and our values. I will teach the Eskimo children their language and history right in the midst of TVs and CBs." She got to her feet and stared out at the water sky and the dark-magenta lead.

"We Iñupiat must do two things to save ourselves from oblivion—change and, at the same time, not change. It is so difficult. Trying to do two things at once makes us confused and sad. It also makes us wonderful. Annie says we can live in two worlds, if we educate ourselves in the white man's ways and do not forget our own.

We must know English to be able to understand what is happening to us and tell the taniks if we don't like it. And we must know all about our culture so we can tell our children its great strengths—that's what Annie says. Annie is very wise. Eskimo for the Eskimo, she always says."

Lincoln awkwardly took her hand. He felt its warmth and delicate bones before she slowly pulled it away.

"Little Owl," he said, "is the Eskimo in me enough? Can I be your Eskimo?"

She cocked her head, took off her sunglasses and smiled at him. Her lips parted like the flower petals of spring. With her face framed in her shimmering gold-and-black wolverine ruff, with her black eyes shining happily, Lincoln felt such love for her that he saw himself doing the seal until his arms broke.

"I have no time for boyfriends. I have too much to do," she answered.

Lincoln lapsed into silence. How was he going to handle this? Kick a ball suspended four feet above his and everyone else's head? —Bounce higher in the blanket-toss contest than an Olympic star on a trampoline? —So high he could touch an eagle?

And then it came to him. He knew what he had to do. Kill a whale. He would be Little Owl's Eskimo if he killed a whale.

"There they are!" she called out excitedly.

"Who?" asked Lincoln, lost in his thoughts of her.

"Our crew." She gave him a look of hopeless tolerance and climbed to a higher piece of ice.

"You could never be an Eskimo," she scolded. "You die in this land if you forget where you are for one moment."

Lincoln heard Roy moan and glanced down at him. He was tied securely, but loosely enough to be comfortable. Suddenly he felt a wave of compassion for Roy. Had it not been for Uncle Jack, he, too, might have been wasted. Uncle Jack had convinced him not to try the drugs the smart guys at school were passing around. Lincoln had been a little bit like Tigluk, getting in and out of trouble until Uncle Jack had showed him something better to do to feel important. He had showed him how to sail the catboat, climb the mountains, paddle the canoe over rapids and find the birds and mammals of the forests and meadows.

"As a matter of fact," Lincoln said to himself, "it was Uncle Jack who taught me how to be an Eskimo. He taught me to respect and love all nature."

Feeling very much an Iñupiat, he proudly slid down the pressure ridge behind Little Owl and started the snow machine.

"Go back and around the ridge," Little Owl said, taking charge of the navigation. "They are over to the right— very close to the water—very close."

Lincoln turned the machine and sled and drove off to the right. He managed several sharp turns by walking back to the sled and yanking it around so it would not tip over. Little Owl kept them on a straight line by kneeling on the seat and keeping several distinctive pieces of ice lined up with the triangular upthrust where she had last seen their crew. She was singing as they rode into the Ologak snow machine parking lot.

As they pulled their sled in to the new campsite, Roy awoke. He moaned and trembled like a wounded bird. Vincent and Weir hurried to meet them, Weir gathering Little Owl up in his arms, Vincent greeting Lincoln with a stern face.

"Do not get separated on the ice," he said, with a sharpness in his voice Lincoln had never heard before. "This is a first law of survival on the ice." He put his head in the tent.

"Bertha, cancel the helicopter. They're here."

Roy moaned.

"Who's that?" Vincent asked.

"Roy," Lincoln answered. "We stopped to rescue him. He was wasted and out of his mind."

"Lincoln had to knock him out," said Little Owl, sensing Vincent's disappointment in Lincoln's performance and this rescue. She tried to smooth things between them. "He was a mess," she said. "He tried to kill Lincoln."

"Little Owl saved my life," Lincoln said, but no one was listening. Bertha had come from the tent to greet the lost two and had discovered the miserable Roy.

"He's suffering," she said, leaning down to touch him. Vincent folded his arms on his chest.

"We must get him back to town," the whaling captain said. "He is a bad spirit."

"I kinda feel sorry for him," Lincoln said, rubbing his neck where Roy's fingers had gripped. "Can't we help him?"

"No." Vincent's voice was a low vibration. "We must all be absolutely in control of ourselves out here on the ice."

Ernie and Utik joined the group around Roy.

"Someone," said Vincent Ologak clearly and slowly, "take Roy to Barrow."

As tightly as the whaling camp was run, it was, nevertheless, a democracy. Every man was the master of his own soul. Although it was wisdom to cooperate, a person was not required to, if he did not think it right. And so no one volunteered to take Roy to town. For a moment Lincoln thought about obeying Vincent Ologak, then decided not to. Whale camp, he knew, was a good place for a boy to be.

The tent fluttered wildly. Vincent Ologak turned like a fox hearing ptarmigan wings. A wind had suddenly hit. He lifted his head into it, sniffed its odor and felt its strength.

"Bad wind." He left Roy and the group and walked to the edge of the lead.

"Bad wind," he repeated, and gazed out on the dark sea. "Do not come yet, old Nukik. The wind makes the water dangerous for the boy."

At Bertha's request Lincoln untied Roy, and he and Kusiq carried him into the tent. Roy's face was bloodied by Lincoln's blow, and he moaned in pain. Little Owl followed them into the tent and put on a pot of tea to soothe everyone's distress.

"How long will he suffer?" Lincoln asked Bertha. She touched his jaw.

"Not long. Roy was once a good student," she continued, ladling melted ice into a bucket. "He comes from a nice family. But his father tries to be a white man. He manages a little company and travels a lot. He does not whale. Whalers keep the best of our traditions. Roy needs to be a whaler. He needs a strong hero—like Vincent."

"A hero?" Lincoln said. "I agree with that all right." He paused. "I had a hero once."

"Once?" Bertha asked carefully, eager not to delve, but to show concern.

"That's why I'm here—in my own mind. To find him. He's the man I asked Vincent about when I first arrived—Uncle Jack James. He came to Barrow and disappeared. He loved the whale. He came to save it."

Bertha dipped a cloth in the bucket of warm water and slowly wrung it out. Gently she wiped Roy's face clean, then dipped the cloth again and let it remain on his forehead to help ease the pain.

"Why doesn't anyone answer me when I mention Uncle Jack's name? Do you know anything about him, Bertha?"

"Yes," she said, peering outside to see where Vincent Ologak was. "He fought with Vincent Ologak long ago. It was a word fight, but a sad one for Vincent Ologak. He liked the young man. Vincent Ologak never speaks of him anymore."

"Where is he?" Lincoln sat up as if he had been hit by a harpoon. "Is he here? Is he in Barrow? Bertha, what do you know about him?" "At long last," Lincoln thought with relief, "someone is talking about Uncle Jack."

"He is all right. That is all I can tell you," Bertha said. "Vincent Ologak must tell you how to find him."

Lincoln lay down to sleep in the twilight of midnight, happy to know Uncle Jack was all right, but not as ecstatic as he had thought he was going to be when he finally found Uncle Jack's trail. Why not? he asked himself, although he already knew the answer. He, Lincoln Noah, had changed. The need to find Uncle Jack was no longer all-consuming. Something had happened inside himself. He was not the same Lincoln Noah Stonewright who had come to Barrow to find an old hero, but a new Lincoln Noah Stonewright—a Lincoln Noah Stonewright who was part Eskimo by birth, a Lincoln Noah Stonewright who was not Eskimo by culture, a Lincoln Noah Stonewright who was part of an old man's dream that a whale would come to him and let itself be taken. And all that had changed how he perceived himself.

"If Roy is mixed up," he mused on, "what am I? I am also part old person and part new person at the same time." Then he grinned. "Now that really makes me a modern Eskimo."

But he also knew that something else had happened and that he was not as confused as it would seem. As the Eskimo put it, he "had become aware." He had a new hero. And it had to be himself. Vincent Ologak and the Eskimo had taught him that.

Another day passed without anyone sighting a whale, then another. On May tenth Lincoln tossed the dish water high in the air behind the tent. It splashed when it hit the ground, and he remembered that the sun would not set tonight. "Spring is here," he said. "That's good. And Uncle Jack is all right. That's good.

"Now to bring Nukik to my people," he thought, and walked toward Weir, who was bending over the umiaq.

"Ukpik," Weir called, using Little Owl's Eskimo name, which he preferred because he had given it to her. Giving a name to a child makes the child very special to the namer. "Come here. We have a crisis." He was bent over the umiaq fingering the skins, which glowed pink in the strong sun. A shaft of light shone through a rip.

"Can you mend this?" he asked. "A seam burst with all the bumping and crashing of the sled."

Vincent saw Weir consulting with Little Owl and joined them.

"Things are going badly," he said, examining the umiaq. "We cannot use this boat."

Ernie came over and studied the rip. "I'll go to Barrow for another skin boat. We cannot go out in this."

"I can fix it, Vincent Ologak," Little Owl said. "But I will need seal fat. Where is the bearded seal you caught?"

"We lost the big ugruk when the ice went out." He turned to Ernie. "You go to Barrow, Ernie. Annie has a strong umiaq in her yard."

[135]

When Ernie had departed for town, Tigluk and Sagniq came down from the perches. They had no reason to watch for whales if there was no boat.

"I can get a seal," Tigluk suddenly offered. "I saw a breathing hole as we came across the ice. It's not far from here. Will that help you, Little Owl?" His father shot him a surprised look.

"It would," she said. Tigluk picked up a spear and an ice chipper and, adjusting the sling on his gun, walked into the wind that was now blowing steadily.

Little Owl took a round basket from her grandfather's sled. It was made of hair-thin strips of baleen. Black and glistening, the basket was intricately woven and beautifully shaped. Lincoln recognized it immediately as quite valuable. His father had brought such a basket home when he had returned as a boy from Barrow. "An investment," he had said of it when Lincoln had inquired. "Baleen baskets are priceless. Most of the Eskimos have forgotten how to make these works of art."

From the basket Little Owl removed a soft piece of sealskin, placed it over the break and cut off a piece to cover it. She sliced with her ulu, the semicircular knife used by the Eskimo women for all cutting jobs, from whale skin to baby hair. After threading the needle, Little Owl studied the rip.

"I see you have caribou tendon for thread," Utik said. "That is rare to see these days."

"I would not use anything else," she replied. "Nylon is not good enough to entrust lives to. It cuts hide." She rolled the edges of the two skins together and began to sew. "Annie made this boat cover. It is made right—with caribou tendon."

The CB crackled. The crew stood at attention. Little Owl stopped stitching.

"Several leads have opened between Wainwright and Barrow. No whales have been sighted." Utik and Sagniq looked at each other in puzzlement. Where was the second run?

"The pack ice is still holding them back," Vincent said. "Good. Maybe things will be better. Nukik will have to wait until the boat is mended. Good." He concentrated his gaze on Tigluk, who stood absolutely motionless at the seal hole, waiting like a wooden totem for the animal to come up to breathe.

An hour passed. The wind blew with more force. Whitecaps danced at the tops of the waves, and Little Owl stitched slowly and neatly. Tigluk stood rigid at the breathing hole.

The ice groaned as the waves rocked it.

Since there were no watches, Lincoln thought about taking a sleep, but changed his mind. Little Owl had done all she could do until she had a seal, and she joined him in the tent. Together they cleaned the pots. Lincoln sharpened one of the whale knives as he had seen Weir do; then he glanced at Tigluk. He was still looking down into the seal hole. Lincoln had never seen anyone stand so still for so long, and despite their differences he admired him very much.

Over the CB came Ernie's voice.

"Tell Vincent Annie loaned her umiaq to her godson. I am trying to track down another. I'll be out as soon as I find one."

Above the call of the wind an *uhhhg* sounded. Tigluk had speared the seal and was struggling to land it. Sagniq and Utik ran to him, and together they pulled an enormous seal through, up, and onto the ice.

Little Owl ran over the ice, dropped to her knees, cut open the seal and took the fat she needed back to the umiaq. She rubbed it into the stitches she had just made. Carefully, she rolled the edges of her seam and, taking tiny stitches, whipped the edges together once more.

"Done," she said, and stood up.

"So that's how you keep out the sea?" Lincoln said with admiration.

"This is very old knowledge," she said. "It is as old as Eskimo whaling."

Softly she tapped Lincoln's arm and pointed to the sun. "The long day begins." The sun did not set.

As Little Owl was returning her basket to Weir's sled, Kusiq brought her a piece of raw seal liver, a delicacy and treat.

"Yum, yum, thank you," she said, and ran to Lincoln, who was still staring at the midnight sun that sat like a fireball above the horizon. "Good food," she said, tapping his shoulder. Smiling, she took a bite, then with her bare hands pressed the same morsel between Lincoln's lips. Her fingers lingered on his mouth as if they were kissing.

He smiled at her with great love. He had seen Bertha feed her beloved Vincent just this way, and he had seen in their eyes what it meant.

"Yum," he said. "From you I like it."

Waldo was on the CB talking from Barrow. "Bertha, I'm waiting for some parts for the printer to come on the afternoon plane. I can't get out until I install them. How can I find you? Over."

"Ernie drove to town. Follow his treads northeast from the crossroads."

Weir looked around the camp. "No Ernie, no Waldo." He counted the rest of the Ologak crew—eight including the owlet and excluding Roy. They could do it nicely.

After a four-hour nap Lincoln picked up his gun and started toward the perch.

"Lincoln Noah," Weir called, "help me test the boat patch." Lincoln suspected he was asking more to test his ability as a boat handler than to test Little Owl's patch.

They slid the umiaq into the choppy water and got in.

"Take the stern," Weir said, and crawled to the bow to kneel over the patch.

After paddling a distance, Weir stood up and clasped his hands above his head.

Little Owl understood his message and clapped.

"The sea stays out," she said to Kusiq, who, grinning with happiness, threw his arms around her and swung her off her feet. "We will get a whale," he said, "thanks to you."

Vincent did not come out of the tent to congratulate Little Owl or, for that matter, to watch the two in the umiaq.

"Nukik!" Weir called out. A great white tail was sinking below the water.

"Nukik!" Lincoln gasped, his skin tingling. Could this be happening? Had he just seen a whale with a white tail? He had. Was it now going to give itself to the great-great-grandson of Nora Ologak? He could not quite believe it.

"Go to shore!" Weir whispered. Lincoln leaned into the paddle and brought the umiaq quietly against the edge of the ice. Without saying a word, Utik, Tigluk, Sagniq and Kusiq took their places. They waited for Vincent. He did not appear. Sagniq ran to the tent to get him and returned quickly.

"Vincent Ologak is sleeping. He has not slept well for so long that Bertha does not want to wake him."

"I'm coming!" Little Owl ran across the ice, stepped into the umiaq and took the seat in front of Lincoln. Weir left Lincoln in the captain's seat. He had seen that he was capable, and there was no time for a change. The whale of Barrow was here.

Lincoln put down his paddle and picked up the steering oar. The crew lifted their paddles, lowered them and stroked as one, sensing each other as do paddlers in Indian war canoes.

Lincoln steered the boat into the wind, calling on both his sailboating and canoeing experience to keep it steady. Wild waves with foamy white-and-green fingers slapped the transparent hides. "The Allagash," he said to himself, "as terrible as it is, was never like this." He steered, following Weir's pointing hand. But sliding over the water, he believed that all the elements—the wind, the current, the sea—were conspiring to protect Nukik, the whale.

They paddled far out into the lead. Thirteen minutes of hard work later, Weir stood up and gestured to a spot in the sea. Lincoln understood his body talk from his experience with Vincent and steered toward the cold, deadly spot where whitecaps hit together and clapped into spray.

The crew slowed their strokes; Lincoln leaned on the oar and steered the umiaq to the spot.

A black hump arose in the middle of the white.

Whoooooosh. Nukik let out his air, spouting water to the very corona of the sun, it seemed to Lincoln. No one moved even though the frozen spray hit them hard across their faces. Lincoln pulled the oar toward the center.

When they were close to the whale, who was now taking short breaths at the surface, the crew held up their paddles and the umiaq slid into the whitecaps. A wave struck them broadside, nearly tipping them over. Another wave sent them sliding sidewise. Lincoln dropped the oar, grabbed his paddle and backwatered. The crew, sensing him, paddled forward on the left, and the umiaq nosed into the waves again. But they were not headed toward the whale.

"Too close," thought Lincoln. "If we keep moving toward the whale from this direction, we'll upset."

Nukik took a short breath and sank below the water.

Weir, who was totally absorbed in the whale, pointed to the next spot where he would emerge. The crew paddled, and Lincoln steered toward it although he knew he should not. The waves were striking them broadside again. He had sailed enough storms with Uncle Jack to know that they were headed for trouble; but no one spoke on the water. If he wanted to go in another direction, he would have to make it known through the silent hunting language of the Eskimo; and he would have to speak through their backs.

Nukik blew after only ten minutes and sounded without taking the short breaths preliminary to a deep dive. Weir pointed, the crew paddled, and Lincoln steered into certain disaster—unless he could change their course. The waves struck broadside; the boat tipped, shipped water and rocked back up. How had Vincent talked to his crew from the rear of the boat without using his voice? Gestures? He thought so.

Weir directed the way to the whale with his hand and arm, selecting the next spot where Nukik would emerge. To reach it they must go broadside to the waves again.

That could not be. Lincoln did what he had to do. He leaned on the oar and steered them—not toward Nukik, but away from him. Weir turned around scowling at his cowardliness. He got *that* message across. But the boat was steady as it headed homeward into the waves. The crew had "heard" Lincoln's message, for they were paddling home with all their strength. They hit a four-foot wave head-on and shot safely over it.

Weir was still standing, his harpoon held high, his whole being concentrated. He wanted the whale.

The wind was kicking up waves so high they were splashing into the boat. Weir paid no attention. He pointed to another spot on the water.

But Lincoln had made up his mind. He continued to steer the boat back to camp. Too many lives were in his hands. It would take only a few minutes in the icy sea to kill them all. Placing the umiaq skillfully beside the edge of the ice—it was a superb boat that did exactly what he wanted it to do—he waited for Weir to chastise him. He did not care. They were safe.

And now he felt the unspoken language of the whale hunters. Weir was stiff with anger and disappointment. The crew, however, were happy. Their relaxed bodies were telling him so. He had made the right decision.

Bertha ran to meet them as they climbed out of the umiaq. Though the wind was a howling wolf pack, and the waves were pyramids of fury, her voice could be heard above them.

"Vincent," she cried. "Vincent Ologak is dying. We must get him to the hospital."

Weir leaped ashore and snatched a sled; Utik ran for one of the snow machines. Lincoln, stunned and bewildered, dropped his oar with a clatter. Little Owl and Kusiq stood as if frozen to the sea ice, and Tigluk fell to his knees. He held his head in his hands.

Vincent Ologak was dying.

NINE

Nauligaun,
the harpoon

THE SLED moved forward. Sagniq drove. Bertha rocked her beloved partner in her arms. Utik stood on the back of the sled. Weir stood alone on the gray ice. As the caravan gained speed, he walked beside his friend, reaching out to him, his face crumpled with grief.

"Vincent wants you," Bertha called over the roar of the engine. "But you must stay. Take the whale."

"Nukik is gone." Weir trotted to keep up. "We lost our chance. He has gone on to the Beaufort." He shook his shaggy head and ran with the sled. "I must go with my friend."

Bertha nodded. Weir grabbed the sled back and swung aboard gracefully beside Utik like the guillemot coming in for a landing. The procession moved more swiftly, tipped as it rounded a green-blue ice boulder, then sped out across the flats. It grew smaller and smaller and vanished behind a pressure ridge. The wailing of the wind seemed full of meaning.

The wind changed suddenly from an offshore blast that was closing the lead to an onshore blow. The ice began to go out with it. Lincoln did not see or feel it. His eyes were squeezed shut to quell the ache inside him. When he could no longer bear it, he slipped away from Little Owl, Kusiq and Tigluk and ran up onto the whale-watching perch. He faced the wild bleakness of the Arctic Ocean that matched the turmoil of his mood.

"Nukik," he heard himself whisper, "if you are really coming to me, wait, please wait. I am without my captain."

The tent flap unzipped and Roy, who had been sleeping off and on since his arrival, walked out into the wind. The gaunt lines in his face had filled out, and but for the bandage on his jaw, he looked like any other attractive young man on a cold adventure.

Roy's Eskimo ancestors had given him broad cheeks, a small flat nose and full, bow-shaped lips. His hair, which was parted in the middle, fell over his forehead like half moons. Roy was husky, his arms and legs slightly short in comparison to his body, as were Vincent's and Weir's and all Eskimos'. Like the polar bear, the lemming, the seal, they had evolved short limbs to conserve body heat. Roy walked with a firm stride to join Little Owl and Kusiq, who were standing in grief by the umiaq. He looked around in bewilderment.

"Where am I?" he asked. He had spoken to no one, not even Bertha, while he recovered. He had just grumbled, eaten and gone back to sleep.

Little Owl brushed the tears from her cheeks. "Be quiet."

"You're in whale camp," Kusiq said listlessly.

"Whale camp?" Roy looked around. "How did I get here?"

"You are in Vincent Ologak's camp," Kusiq went on. "He is ill. He is dying. He . . . " But Kusiq could say no more.

"Vincent Ologak dying?" Roy said. "He can't do that."

Kusiq turned away, picked up the oar Lincoln had dropped and placed it in the boat. The burning sadness in his throat would not stop. He thought he might quench it by doing chores—anything. He rewound the walrus rope on the float and checked nauligaun, the harpoon. But he still hurt. His beloved elder was dying.

Little Owl saw his pain and put her hand soothingly on his arm. He smiled but, unable to look at her without crying, looked away and asked her to help him pull the umiaq up onto the ice. She, too, needed to be busy. Gratefully Little Owl grabbed a gunwale, and together they pulled the skin boat up on the ramp. Little Owl examined the patch she had made, then checked the gunwales by running her hands along them. Her mitten snagged on a small crack in the wood. A weak gunwale was serious, but this one was welcome. It gave her an excuse to talk about something other than that which was eating her heart like gulls on a kill.

"I must fix this," she said to Kusiq. Their eyes met, and Little Owl's tears welled up and spilled down her cheeks. Lincoln did not turn around. He could hear her crying, and he, too, cried for the wonderful man who had done so much for them all. Presently, Lincoln heard Little Owl speaking in Iñupiat and looked down. She was patting the ice with her sealskin mittens. Kusiq, knees bent, hands to one side of his body, was somberly dancing, a gentle dance to drive their grief away. As Lincoln watched them call upon old Eskimo traditions in this crisis, he knew that as much as he would like to be part of his Arctic family, he would never be more than a visitor from the outside. He did not know the ancient languages.

He turned back to the lashing water and searched for the spout of Nukik, a spout as distinctive to him now as the white tail.

After a timeless interlude he heard Little Owl speak in English.

"Do you know how to strengthen a weak gunwale, Kusiq? Ataata always fixes the frames."

"Bind a piece of wooden slat from one of the sleds to the broken gunwale like a splint with your caribou tendon. I'll saw off a piece." He turned away. "Roy, come help."

Roy did not move. "Who is that?" he asked, catching a glimpse of Lincoln's pale forehead.

"Lincoln Noah Stonewright," Kusiq answered.

"Tanik. What's a white man doing in whale camp?"

"You've already had it out with him once, Roy," Kusiq said. "And he beat you up—badly."

"I had it out with him?" Roy's expression was blank. No memory search brought up the image of a fight. "I had it out with him, that weakling? And he beat me up?"

"Feel your jaw."

Roy reached up and flinched as he touched his sore chin.

"He saved your life, by the way. You had dumped your machine and were wasted on the ice. He and Little Owl happened to find you."

"Dumped my machine?"

"You were a mess."

"Where is Bertha? The Health Office said she would take care of me."

"Roy," Little Owl said, "we're all busy out here. The village is depending on us. You just go sit somewhere and stay out of trouble."

"Bertha promised to help me."

"This is whale camp. Do you understand? We don't help. We cooperate. This spot has been made sacred by our love for each other. Now go. I agree with Vincent Ologak. You should not be here."

A loud report like a rifle shot rang out. The ice moved and a crack appeared behind the tent. Kusiq looked at the now quiet water, and threw up a handful of snow. The wind was offshore.

"Roy," he said, "we're in trouble. We've broken free. We are being blown to sea. There is only one snow machine. Go get it." He pointed. "Bring it back and hitch all the sleds to it. We're getting out of here.

"Off the ice!"

Lincoln jumped down from the perch, picked up a hammer and had knocked the tent spikes onto the ice by the time Roy had arrived with the snow machine, jumped off and hitched the sleds to it, one behind the other.

Little Owl loaded the stoves and food box. Tigluk packed the tent while Roy and Lincoln put the plywood floorboards onto a sled. Little Owl and Tigluk tied on the whale knives. The ice floe twisted slowly.

"Now the umiaq," Lincoln called.

"We don't have time," said Little Owl. She pointed to the water surging up through another wide crack between them and the boat. Kusiq started the engine.

"Weir's harpoon and lance are in it," Lincoln cried over the wind. "We can't leave that!"

"Leave it," Little Owl urged. "It is not worth your life."

Lincoln had done more reckless things than jump an ice crack to save a boat in his life. He leaped the crack, grabbed the boat painter and yanked. It did not budge. He yanked harder. Suddenly the skin boat was sliding as if driven by a motor, and he glanced around to see Roy pushing from behind. He had leaped the crack to help.

"Heave, heave, heave," Lincoln shouted, and the umiaq slid to the crack.

"Too late," he said when he saw how wide it had become. "We can't jump that and pull the boat across. We're afloat." He turned around and looked out across the widening lead.

Roy cried like a deserted wolf pup.

"Shut up!" Lincoln snapped. The ice slab rocked. The water turned into surf and boiled up over their boots.

"Help! Help!" Roy yelled as he swung his arms in panic. He was totally out of control. Lincoln ran around the bow of the umiaq and slapped him sharply across the face. Roy stopped screaming.

"That's better," Lincoln said. "Grab a side. Push the boat into the water, get in and paddle. We're all right. We have a boat. It's time you help yourself."

Roy grabbed the gunwales, and as the bow hit the water he scrambled in. When the stern was afloat, Lincoln leaped, and they were launched. Roy glanced at Lincoln to see how he held the paddle, imitated his grip and dug the water. The wind helped them cross the lead while at the same time drenching them with sea spray that instantly froze on their hair and snow shirts. Icicles formed on their sunglasses, but they did not see or feel them. Lincoln and Roy were paddling for their lives, headed out across the lead, driving for the other side.

"You're going the wrong way," Roy shouted.

"Paddle!" Lincoln yelled, and steered the boat with the wind and current. The umiaq rode like a spear through the sea.

"Don't stop paddling until the wind dies," Lincoln yelled. "Just keep it up, and we'll be all right." Although the spray was freezing on their mittens and parkas, they were actually hot from exertion inside their insulated cocoons.

Now and then Roy vanished behind the spray; but he paddled. He paddled hard, as if, at last, he understood that his life depended on his doing something for himself. He would paddle if he had to paddle to Siberia. No one else could do it for him.

Little Owl, Kusiq and Tigluk waited until they saw Lincoln and Roy get into the umiaq and head out across the lead; then Little Owl drove the snow machine, and Tigluk and Kusiq pushed the long line of sleds from behind. Slowly they crossed the crackling pan ice. When they reached thicker ice, they paused and looked back. Lincoln and Roy were still paddling—very much alive and safe.

Lincoln glanced at them and noted that they were winding north. He bent over his paddle and worked.

Almost as suddenly as the wind had struck, it died, in keeping with its unpredictable reputation. Lincoln and Roy slowed their pace. The sun that was up for the summer was warming the sea, melting the ice and slowing down the wind. They paddled until anugI lost its momentum and the lead became as smooth as glass.

"Okay. Take five," said Lincoln, and clunked his paddle across the gunwale and rested heavily upon it. Roy collapsed over his knees.

The umiaq traveled on with the current, headed toward the other side of the lead. But the danger was over. It was now only a matter of paddling back in the calm sea.

After a long rest Lincoln scanned the land-fast ice for

his friends. There was no sign of them anywhere—gone to safety, he hoped.

"Okay, Roy," he said. "We're turning around. Paddle on the left. I'll backwater on the right."

In the icy silence a great darkness moved below them. Rising slowly, it broke the surface. A geyser spouted to the sun.

"Nukik," Lincoln whispered, "is that you?"

Roy drew to the far side of the boat.

"He'll upset us," he whined. "Get us out of here."

"Be still."

The whale breathed in, then out, then in and out again. Through the crystal water Lincoln could see the white on the bowhead's lower lip, which protruded beyond the upper. He could see a scar on the back.

"Nukik!" he said. "Hi. Thanks for waiting." He could not see the tail or the eyes set low and far back in the head, but he knew Nukik was looking up at him, for he tilted as if gazing up with one eye. Was he curious about him, too? What did Nukik see? Did he see Lincoln Noah Stonewright, the great-great-grandson of Nora Ologak? Lincoln did not think so—and yet—there were great mysteries out here in this indigo-and-green water. There were events that people who were dependent upon farms and stores and land would never know because they did not need to. Out here where water and ice ruled life, Lincoln could believe as the Eskimos do—that mankind and the animals are part of each other; that all life is interdependent; and that a whale was coming to him.

Nukik breathed in and tucked his head. His island-sized back came into view, scarred by icebergs and possibly whale battles, perhaps even encounters with ships. The huge whale rolled to his side, waved a flipper and slapped it against the water.

"Wait, Nukik," Lincoln called softly. "Vincent Ologak will get well. He will get well."

"Ah, u!" said Roy, his eyes wide as an owl's as he watched the whale of Barrow town.

The track Nukik left was gigantic and as smooth as a parking lot, as slick as an oil spill, and was rimmed with snapping bubbles.

"Awesome fellow," Lincoln whispered.

On the other side of the whale print skimmed the Rudd crew. They had seen Nukik when the wind had died down and were after him as fast as they could paddle.

"Wait, Nukik," Lincoln called to the empty track as he backwatered with all his strength. "Paddle, Roy. Let's find our crew."

As they passed the Rudds, they tipped their paddles in greeting, but under his breath Lincoln growled, "Go home, Otis Rudd. That whale is coming to me."

Lincoln and Roy pulled up to what they thought was their former campsite only to find a bleak scene. Where the tent had sat was a bay of crystal water, and shining sheets of new ice stretched between gray floes where they had once laughed and watched for Nukik.

"Now what?" asked Lincoln.

"Follow the ice edge," Roy said. "That's what everyone says, isn't it? Eskimos follow the ice edge. Well, I guess that's what Kusiq will do."

"Good thinking," said Lincoln, and together they paddled along the edge of the lead going in the direction Lincoln had seen his crewmates take.

They rounded a chunk of iceberg and entered a cove. The water was glassy calm and a joy to see, but what looked even better to the tired paddlers was the pan ice. It was solid enough to hold a town.

"Let's get out here," Lincoln said. "We can climb that pressure ridge and look for our crew."

When the umiaq was up on the ice, Roy chipped a hole with his knife, stuck his paddle in it and ripped his red handkerchief in half. He tied it to the paddle.

"So we can find the boat," he said. "I'll mark our trail with strips from the other half."

"You are really thinking today," said Lincoln, and led the way up the pressure ridge.

On top they could see to the gray, ominous pack ice to the north. To the southwest glittered the lead where Nukik swam, and to the east and north blue and green and blinding white ice moved and changed like pieces in a kaleidoscope. Lincoln was spellbound.

"Don't see them," said Roy. "Maybe we should paddle to Rudd's camp and use their CB. I'm sure Tigluk has set ours up wherever he is."

"No," said Lincoln. "Let's keep looking. They've got to be near." Slowly he made a complete circle, but could see only the blue lead and the glints and flashes of the sun on the ice. He felt light-headed and dizzy. The ice wilderness was playing tricks on his brain.

And then he snapped out of it. The Rudd crew was out in the lead. He reached for his binoculars. They were paddling home and they flew no flag to say that a whale had been taken. Nukik was alive.

Roy worked his way across a deep fissure and climbed to the top of the highest pinnacle. Carefully he unfolded himself and stood up. He scanned the ice.

"I see them! I see them!" He pulled off his frozen snow shirt and waved it in the air. Lincoln scrambled up beside him. They both waved. No one looked up. They shouted. No one heard.

Finally, Roy stuck his fingers in his mouth and whistled shrilly. The sound sent vibrations into the ice and started a small avalanche, but they did not notice. They were concentrating on the snow machine, the four sleds, and the tiny figures climbing a distant part of the same pressure ridge, obviously to search for them.

Then the whistle reached Little Owl's ears. She pulled back her parka hood, the better to hear and, lifting her binoculars, scanned the horizon. She saw them.

"Stay there," she signaled. "We're coming."

In less than an hour the young Ologak whalers were laughing together in the cove where the umiaq sat.

"Now what do we do?" Lincoln asked.

"Set up camp and get the whale of Barrow town," said Roy.

Kusiq grinned at Roy. Little Owl grinned at Roy. Tigluk turned all the way around and grinned at Roy; and Lincoln opened his mouth and stared as the obvious hit him.

"Of course, that's exactly what we do," he said. "We get the whale of Barrow town."

TEN

Nutagaq, the young whalers

THE YOUNG WHALERS pitched their tent under a sun that sat like a silver ball above the top of the world. The weather was ideal for whaling. The sea was a silver mirror and no wind stirred.

Gulls circled the campsite looking for food, and seals popped up in the cove to look at the people. A walrus hauled himself up on an ice floe and sat chest out, head up, like a warrior defending his domain, which was exactly what he was doing. He was feeling crowded by the seals and the whalers.

The cove made an excellent whaling campsite. The new ice was thick, and the cove waters were surrounded by pressure ridges from which the whalers could see almost the entire lead.

Lincoln appointed himself first watch person after the tent went up. He chipped steps up a mound of pale-blue ice and took his post, scanning the water like the walrus. And this he knew, as he looked out on the sleek water: Nukik had waited.

Inside the tent Kusiq and Tigluk were not so happy. The CB was wet, and it would neither broadcast nor receive. The young whalers were desperate to contact the hospital to ask about Vincent Ologak and, now that they were all together, to tell someone where they were. But the equipment was silent. Kusiq placed the CB near the kerosene heating stove, hoping it would dry out and work. From time to time he felt it to see if it was getting dry.

"I think the kerosene heat is too hot and uneven," he said to Tigluk. "I'll get some fat from the patching seal and make a lamp. Seal oil's best for drying."

"Little Owl's patching seal went out with the ice," Tigluk said.

Kusiq remembered Bertha had saved a piece of the seal meat, so he took a roast from the food box and carved off some fat. He melted it in a pan and cut off a piece of his undershirt for a wick. He lit this, and a tall flame leaped into existence and burned steadily.

Roy had fallen onto the sleeping skins as soon as they were spread and now, several hours later, was lying awake, slowly becoming aware that Kusiq and Tigluk were in the tent. He rolled to his elbow.

"You should've seen me paddle big huge waves," he said. "They came at me like monsters. They clawed like polar bears."

Tigluk and Kusiq were concentrating on the CB and did not hear him.

"It was hard to move that umiaq," Roy went on. "It

was also dangerous. I was almost washed into the sea, but I thought, 'No, my people need this boat.' " Tigluk had taken the case off the CB and was wiping some of the parts. Kusiq placed the glowing seal-oil lamp near the radio.

"We've *got* to get through to the hospital," he said.

Roy had no audience. He shrugged, got up—they all slept with their clothes on—saw the food box and opened it. Taking out a leg of frozen caribou, he put it in a pot, covered it with the salt-free ice and placed it on the stove. Before long the tent filled with the odor of mouth-watering caribou stew simmering in its juices. He perked a pot of coffee and was pleased with himself.

Outside the tent Little Owl had stacked ice blocks into a ramp and asked Lincoln to come down from his perch and help her pull the umiaq up on it. When he went back on watch, she checked Weir's harpoon, float and lance, and was relieved to find them undisturbed. She made sure all the paddles were in place, then she climbed the blue ice steps to Lincoln.

"Lincoln," she said, "we have no leader.

"Since you have sat in the stern and since you make good decisions, I, as the granddaughter of the second-most-important person, the harpooner, make you captain." Lincoln kept his eyes on the water as he considered her astonishing words.

"What about the others? Don't we vote?"

"We all agree. Captains must be leaders—fearless, powerful and intelligent; also wealthy. That's you." Lincoln's heart beat more strongly at her flattering words, and he wanted to say something clever. She went on before he could think of a remark.

"The captain's wife is the manager. That's me." Lincoln smiled at their being captain and wife. Reading his thoughts, she went on in a businesslike manner.

"Here's what I propose.

"Our problems are many. The CB is busted. We must know how Vincent Ologak is, and we must tell Weir and the others how to find us.

"*Then* . . . " She took a deep breath. "We must take Nukik for Vincent Ologak," she said. "But we need Weir.

"Since all our problems could be solved with a CB, I'll take the machine and go down to Rudd's camp. I'll call Annie. She'll do the rest."

"You can't go to Rudd's camp," he said, not knowing quite why. "I'll go."

"No, no. The whale is coming to you. He will stay if he sees you."

"The whale is also out there for anyone to take. The Rudd crew has been paddling around since I came on watch. Nukik blows. They paddle to the spot where they think he'll come up. He does not. He blows somewhere else, usually behind them. They don't seem to know much about whales."

"They know a lot about whales all right," Little Owl said. "But Nukik *is* waiting for you. He has stayed in this lead for two days. That is not what migrating whales do. They go on and on—unless they want to be taken." Lincoln glanced across the marine-blue water. Out here in the constant daylight, out here on a footing that would soon turn to water, the Eskimo belief that a whale comes to a person to be killed seemed right and beautiful and more civilized than just killing for food.

A flock of eider ducks flew up over the ice block, veered when they saw Lincoln and Ukpik and winged on, chattering like a crowd of irritated people. Three bow-shaped guillemots flew behind them.

"Little Owl," Lincoln said after a bit, "have you ever thrown a harpoon? Did Weir ever teach you?"

Ukpik, the owlet, took a deep breath and thought about whether or not she should answer.

"Yes," she finally said. "Women usually do not learn such things. But Weir has taught me everything because I am writing it all down—to preserve the old whaling techniques—all the details. To do this work well, I have to learn to do everything. I have thrown the harpoon."

"What did you throw it at?"

"Old sealskins with dots on them."

"Did you hit the spots?"

"Yes."

"Could you be our harpooner?"

"I am not strong enough."

Lincoln did not take his eyes from the lead, where the Rudd crew were now following the gulls to Nukik.

"But I can teach *you*," Little Owl said.

Lincoln stuffed his mittened hands deep into the big pockets on the front of his snow shirt, now dirty white. He rose up and down on his toes.

"Once I thought I could kill a whale for my people,"

he said slowly, knowing that as he spoke, he was losing Little Owl's respect. No matter how long he held the seal position or how high he went in the blanket toss, this beautiful person could not admire a man who could not kill a whale. "Now I know I cannot."

"Then you could use the shoulder gun," she said, not wishing to understand him. "It is quite easy, even if it does kick like a moose."

Lincoln watched the gulls wheeling in growing numbers over the Rudd crew.

"That is not the problem, Little Owl. It's that I cannot kill a whale."

"But you are an Eskimo, Karuk."

"Only because my great-great-grandmother was Eskimo. I was raised a tanik—and I think like a tanik. I cannot kill a whale. But I want you to."

"Oh, Lincoln Noah," Ukpik said softly, "the whale does not die. It becomes part of us; our bodies, our festivals, our art. It lives. You shall see." But all Lincoln could see was the lovely person beside him and the disappointment in her face. How he longed to please her, but how well he knew he could not.

"You are strong. You struck down the beautiful polar bear. You must kill the whale of Barrow town. He is coming to you."

"The bear was going to kill Tigluk. I had no problem with that."

"The whale is coming to you," she repeated. "You must kill him."

The sunlight struck at a lower angle and changed the sea from steely silver to emerald green. Lincoln tried to push Little Owl's words out of his head. He thought of home and school. He thought of Uncle Jack and his dreams of saving the bowhead from extinction.

But the words "You must kill the whale of Barrow town" crept in. He thought about his love for Vincent Ologak; his admiration for Weir Amaogak; his kinship with his fellow survivors, Kusiq and Tigluk and Little Owl—even with Roy, who had crossed the expanding crack to help him.

To himself he said: "I am not the same person who stepped off the jet at the Barrow airport. But I am not an Eskimo either."

He could not kill a whale.

Kusiq came up the glassy steps and sat down on a chunk of ice.

"Is Nukik still out there?" he asked.

An answer came from the sea—the water whorled downward to form a sleek funnel. The funnel reversed itself into a cone and exploded into droplets. Nukik's giant blowhole appeared above the surface, the white mark on its surface emerging into the sunlight. With a roaring *whoosh* he sprayed the young Ologak crew with purple-green diamonds. His beak rose out of the water, then his great twenty-foot mouth that curved upward toward the top of his head and down again in a perpetual smile. He lifted himself still higher. Nukik's eye leveled with Lincoln's eye. A black pupil in a gold-green iris met

Lincoln's black pupil. The whale eye was kind. Lincoln's knees trembled. Nukik rose up until his tail stock was visible. He was tremendous, all blue-black and stream-lined like a tear. He twisted a flipper.

"Praise the Lord," whispered Little Owl.

"Lotsa maktak," said Kusiq.

"I can't," said Lincoln.

The whale threw himself backward almost gleefully, sending sheets of water like tidal waves to either side. They broke into surf. The surf washed up over the new ice, splashed the umiaq and rolled back into the sea.

Nukik lay for a moment on his side, then back dived into the sparkling water. The last thing the young crew saw of him was his handsome white tail, and they could not speak.

"The Rudd crew!" Kusiq whispered. "They're after our whale."

"Whale! Man the boat!" Lincoln called.

Roy and Tigluk dashed out of the tent, struggling into their parkas. The crew assembled at the umiaq and took hold of the gunwales.

"Heave!"

The umiaq slipped quietly into the water.

"We have only a harpoon and a lance," Lincoln said as he took his place in the stern.

"That's all we need," whispered Little Owl.

"Stop!" a voice called from the ice shore. "Wait for me!"

Lincoln turned to see a bulky man in white, with a

rifle slung around him, binoculars hanging from his neck. His face was rimmed with a splendid yellow beard under his dark glasses. He leaped into the umiaq, stepped over the seats and picked up Weir's harpoon.

"Musk Ox," Kusiq said. "Wow, what are you doing here?"

"Tanik," snarled Tigluk.

"Stroke!" ordered Lincoln. The boat slipped away from the ice and skimmed over the calm sea.

The Rudd crew had moved near the edge of the pack ice and were waiting for Nukik to blow.

Lincoln knew that Nukik had made a back dive and figured that the whale would come up to the east, not the west. He steered toward the eastern end of the lead. The Rudds paddled west, and in moments they were far apart.

Twenty minutes passed. Nukik did not come up. Musk Ox shook his head; even Lincoln knew by now that thirteen minutes was an average time for a whale to be submerged, but he also knew some could stay under for thirty minutes. He held the boat where it was and waited.

The crew was motionless as they watched Lincoln out of the corners of their eyes. He put down his paddle and picked up the rudder oar. The crew paddled gently. Lincoln lifted his oar. Even with their backs to him, they sensed the oar's position and stopped paddling.

The gulls climbed high in the sky to get a better view of the fish Nukik was stirring to the surface. The seals poked up their heads and watched the people curiously.

An old male slapped his tail in warning. All dived out of sight.

Musk Ox leaned down and scooped up a handful of water and examined it. Lincoln studied the water beneath him. It was dark with life. Minute animals, making a soup as thick as oatmeal, drifted with the current. Here and there he caught glints of light that were tiny glassy eyes.

He longed to ask Musk Ox, the leader of the science camp, about the animals below him, but he was whaling; he had to be silent. He watched the water.

"Whale!" he gasped. He leaned hard on the oar. The crew paddled. A smaller blow erupted near the first.

"Mother and baby," Little Owl signaled. Lincoln lifted his oar. The Ologak crew stopped paddling as the Rudd crew sped toward the pair as swiftly as the jaeger, the predatory gull.

Lincoln backwatered, his crew paddled and the boat turned around. With an *ugh* he started them off toward the west side of the lead, leaving the Rudd crew to come eastward to look for the mother and baby. They would not find her, Lincoln knew. He had seen her dive under the ice as she went east toward the Beaufort Sea.

Nukik surfaced close to the Rudd crew and, as if to divert them from the mother and baby, breached and hung above them. Or perhaps, Lincoln thought, he is breaching to see if the big and little whale tracks lead under the ice to safety. Whatever he was doing, he fell back with a *splash* that nearly swamped the Rudd umiaq.

Lincoln steered his crew west, away from Nukik.

Musk Ox turned around, took off his sunglasses and glowered. His expression said, "What are you doing, for heaven's sake?"

Lincoln rose to his feet, almost losing command of the boat. The eyes, the eyes, the eyes; the long pinched nose, the prominent cheek and brow bones. A person was announcing himself.

"Uncle Jack?" Lincoln mouthed the name.

The golden beard framed a big grin and flashing white teeth. The shaggy head nodded.

Lincoln plunked back into his seat. He could not believe it. Uncle Jack had dropped from the sun into his boat—and probably just in time.

The Rudd crew, having lost the mother and baby, had turned around and were paddling toward the Ologak crew. They came on fast with their complement of twelve whalers—Lincoln could think no more about Uncle Jack.

Nukik's next blow was long and drawn out, as if he were thinking as he exhaled. He hung at the surface, like a volcanic island, black and cone shaped.

"This is it." Lincoln's voice seemed to come from somewhere outside his body. "This is it."

The umiaq skipped like a skimmer bird over the water, for like that bird, it was the perfect creation for its purpose, and it approached the whale without disturbing the water and in silence. Nukik took a breath and submerged, came up and lay on the top of the water—to give himself to those young whalers? They thought so.

The Rudd crew was within earshot. A whale belonged to anyone until harpooned, and then it belonged to the harpooner's crew even if it was killed by another.

Lincoln did not want to be rushed by the Rudds and set the pace faster to gain a little distance. The Ologak crew was young and strong, and they moved their boat along swiftly. The whale waited.

Little Owl lifted the harpoon as they approached him. When they were beside his great beak, she handed the weapon to Musk Ox. He nodded and took it. He understood. Little Owl tilted and aimed it for him. She aimed it out of kindness. She aimed it with two thousand years of knowledge behind her.

The Rudd crew closed in. Their harpooner raised a shoulder gun and pointed it at Nukik. He was not going to use a harpoon, just shoot the gun. He was going for an instant kill, running the risk of wounding the whale.

Without a harpoon and float attached, a wounded whale could get away and would eventually die. The Rudd crew were indeed radical Eskimos. They did not even respect their own unwritten law to use harpoons. Lincoln was furious. A whale was too regal for such desperate shooting.

Musk Ox held the harpoon where Little Owl had aimed it. Then suddenly he turned, pulled Kusiq to his feet and gave the harpoon to him.

Kusiq took it eagerly, and with a loud grunt threw it. The harpoon hit the mark and disappeared. The whale plunged.

The line ran out; Little Owl tossed the sealskin float onto the water. After what seemed to be three thousand years the whale came to the surface. The crew paddled up to him. Kusiq now picked up the jade-tipped lance. He held it above his head, aimed and, with the skill of the professional he was, thrust it deep into the whale. There was a sigh from the nostrils. The whale rolled over belly up in death. The gift was given.

"Hallelujah."

"AġviQ qaitchuq," Tigluk said. "The whale gave itself."

Little Owl got to her feet and pressed her hands to her chest.

"Forgive me, great aġviQ. I pray for your spirit. May it enter into Vincent Ologak and give him peace as he dies. May it enter my people and bring us together again. May it fly out over the sea and bring health and new life to your people, the whales. Thank you, brave whale. Amen."

The Rudd crew bowed their heads.

"AġviQ," Captain Otis Rudd said, "enter our lives in the name of Vincent Ologak. Amen." He sat down and steered his umiaq to the Ologak boat, reached across the gunwales and clasped hands with Kusiq. Tears ran freely down his face.

"Praise the Lord. Amen," said Captain Rudd. The crews stood up and hugged each other, laughing and cheering. The whale of Barrow town belonged to them all. Lincoln, torn between great sadness and great joy, had to believe what he was seeing. The two fighting crews were friends.

A whale had given itself.

ELEVEN

Aitchuusiaq, the sea gift

THE SMILES on the faces of the crews became thankfulness, the thanks became hallelujahs, the hallelujahs tripped over into song. Gulls heard and circled the singers, searching for the food they must be celebrating. Lincoln could see the red of their eyes and sense the single-minded fishing intelligence that led them to their food. The seals, feeling the commotion through vibrations in the water, gathered around the whale in pairs and herds. They hunted the sea gifts the bowhead had churned up for them in death. A walrus pulled up on a floe of ice and barked in annoyance. The great white whale fluke had swirled him up from his clamming on the sea bottom. He roared.

Little Owl laughed as she held on to the Rudd umiaq. She had pushed her sunglasses up and her lovely face was sparkling with sweat and spray and a joy Lincoln could not really understand.

"See what nice people the Rudds are?" she said to him over her shoulder. "I told you so."

"Hey, you didn't say that at all!" He stared at her in wonder. The whale had, indeed, effected a change. He wondered if Otis Rudd now liked Vincent Ologak and Vincent Ologak liked Otis Rudd, and what about Vincent and Roy, and himself, Tigluk and Roy? Had Bertha and Vincent forgotten their spat?

"Whatever's happening, it's nice," he said to himself. A flock of old-squaw ducks separated, flew around the whalers and came back together. They sped on toward the rivers, where the ice was beginning to break up and the water to flow again.

"The geese will be arriving next," Little Owl said wistfully, watching the ducks go by. "And we'll all go inland to hunt niglivIk, the white-fronted goose, along the rivers. We need a great variety of tasty flavors for Nalukataq."

The Rudd crew cut off the flukes, and four men hoisted one.

"For the successful captain to distribute," Rudd called as his men tossed the fluke into the Ologak boat—nearly upsetting it, to the laughter of all. The second one followed the first.

The Rudd harpooner then fastened a line to the bowhead's tail stock and tied a tow rope to that. Little Owl tied their boat line to the tow rope and to the rear of Vincent Ologak's umiaq. She chattered and laughed at everything, including the icicles on Musk Ox's beard and Kusiq's remark about the coffee she made. When the whale was secure, the Rudd crew tied up to the tow rope.

Sensing he was not needed, Lincoln kept out of their

way, thereby giving himself time to absorb the fact that he was sitting in an umiaq in the Arctic Ocean with Uncle Jack. But for the ice, the whale, the walrus, and a long list of Eskimo names, they were back together again doing what they loved to do—matching their wits with and learning from nature.

"Hey," he suddenly said to himself, "I'm no longer hurt and angry. I was going to give that man a tiger blow when I met him. I was going to grumble at him for not writing. But I feel good—just wonderful." He rubbed his fuzzy chin. "Could it be? Could it really be?" Lincoln turned around and looked at the whale.

And he stopped musing. They were drifting away from the cove. The once-still water was scalloped with lacquer-smooth waves. A wind lifted a tuft of loose wolverine underfur from his ruff and blew it away from the cove.

"It's going to be tough paddling," he said to Roy, who was sitting in front of him.

"You and I have paddled in worse than this," Roy answered cheerfully.

"The sea, it seems," Lincoln mused, "wants to keep its gift."

"Indian giver," Roy blurted, then caught himself. Slurs about any group were out of place now. Even he felt that.

Kusiq hoisted Vincent Ologak's flag.

"Hallelujah!" cheered both crews.

"Let's go, Linc," called Jack.

Lincoln stood up and, selecting a land-fast ice sculpture in the distance, which he recognized as one of their perches, steered the boat toward it. In the hour it had taken to secure the whale, the camp had become a pinhead on the pale-blue ice. He looked down at the water. The current had changed. Once more sagvaq, the current, and anugI, the wind, were fighting them.

But it mattered not. The paddlers were inspired. The famine of the body and spirit was over. The Ologak and Rudd crews were bringing a whale to the people of Barrow town, and they would fight the current and the wind to do it.

"Hallelujah!" Lincoln called. "Stroke!"

They all paddled and sang with such joy that Lincoln knew that for the moment, at least, it did not matter that he and Uncle Jack were from the outside.

"Niqislauraq, niqislauraq," (a lot of food), the Rudd crew sang.

"AġviQ, aġviQ," Kusiq sang out, his face smudged with sweat and whale grease.

"Great aġviQ, you have given yourself to us.

"Great whale, you waited for me.

"This harpooner has set your spirit free.

"This harpooner will live your life on land."

The Ologak crew waited through his solo, then opened up their hearts on the chorus. In Iñupiat they sang:

"I understand myself when I see the whale.

"He is I. I am he.

"I understand who I am when I see the whale.

"He is I. I am he.

"All the living things are reflected in his eye.

"I am the eye of the whale."

Lincoln was lost. The song was beautiful and he could sense its meaning, but he did not know for sure. Uncle Jack turned around and smiled to say that he, too, was left out.

Kusiq sang another stanza of the harpooner's song in English.

The Rudd crew came in with Iñupiat on the chorus, and as they sang, Lincoln knew he was not, and never could be, an Eskimo. He was doomed forever to be an outsider. That he would not kill a whale certainly kept him on the outside, but there were many Eskimos who did not kill whales. No, it was their songs that drew a circle around them and left him out. The songs were root music. They had been passed down from whaler to whaler for thousands of years. They bound enemy to enemy and made them friends. Even if he learned the words and music, he still would be on the outside of the circle because, he knew, he could never sing with the deep feelings for "giving" that he had been hearing. Lincoln had never suffered for want of a whale to share.

The wind strengthened. The boats rocked. Water sloshed up the sides of the umiaqs and soaked the paddlers' hands. They laughed and paddled harder. The whale caravan inched forward.

After a long effort, Otis Rudd waved to get Lincoln's attention.

"The current and wind are strange," he called. "The sky is clear. The current takes us out. The wind blows us in."

The waves crested and slapped the gunwales as if to emphasize the problem. Lincoln stepped up the cadence. They had to reach camp before too much water sloshed into the umiaqs and swamped them.

The tent grew smaller, not larger.

"Uncle Jack," Lincoln called, "we're losing ground."

Musk Ox turned around. Lincoln was diverted once more by his eyes. He would know them anywhere—they were like his mother's eyes, a clear pale blue with penetrating black pupils. The huge golden beard made them shine more brightly. Lincoln grinned at his uncle. His kinsman grinned at him.

"What are your orders, sir?" Jack asked. "This thing weighs fifty tons, and fifty tons is a lot to move against a wind."

"Should we quarter the waves?" Lincoln asked. "If you and I could quarter the waves in that tub we sailed through the nor'easter, we can quarter 'em with this freighter."

"Aye, aye, sir. We can. And I think we should."

Lincoln stood up, tossed up a piece of underfur and noted the wind direction. He studied the bubbles on the water and saw the direction the current was flowing. Still standing, he leaned against the oar-rudder and, recalling his canoeing experiences, angled the umiaq into the waves, changing their direction. He gestured to Otis Rudd to do the same. Otis Rudd shook his head to tell Lincoln he was pointed the wrong way. Both crews saw the conflict of captains, but the Rudd crew stopped paddling. They were not going to budge without the consent of their umialik, their captain.

"Now what do I do?" Lincoln asked himself. "How do I get this strong-minded man to follow?" Otis was shaking his fist and pointing the other way. He was also digging the air to say that only brute force would get them home.

Lincoln thought a moment.

"Kusiq," he said. "Let me borrow your watch." Quickly the gadgety instrument was passed to him. Its buttons and dials were prominent enough to be seen by Otis.

Holding the watch on his open palm, he pointed his hand toward the sun, into the wind, with the current, then studied the watch, trying to recall how to set off the alarm.

"The red button," Kusiq said when he saw what Lincoln was up to.

The alarm buzzed shrilly.

"That way!" Lincoln pointed the way he wanted to go. "Paddle!"

Nobody moved. Lincoln began to sweat as he realized what he had thoughtlessly done. He had treated Otis Rudd like an ignorant savage. He closed his eyes, not wishing to see the hurt in his face.

Laughter; he heard laughter from Otis Rudd. He opened his eyes.

"You're a good clown," Rudd called. "I like you all right." His crew chuckled good-humoredly.

"That way," Otis Rudd said, pointing in the direction

Lincoln had indicated. Lincoln smiled gratefully at Otis Rudd and knew the spirit of the whale was upon them.

When they were quartering the waves, the water shoved against the rear of the boats and the whale and pushed them forward with more speed than paddling alone could do. Gradually they crossed the lead and, because of the angle they were on, overshot the Ologak camp by almost a quarter of a mile.

"Think we should take it back now, Uncle Jack?"

"I do."

"Right side, backwater. Left side, paddle. Hard. Hard. Hard." The umiaqs shivered, turned and moved obliquely back toward the cove, and again the wind and the current shoved the caravan along.

After a long paddle, Lincoln wondered how long they'd been out in the ocean. The sun, as usual, was in the sky, but of no use to him in telling the time. He guessed that they must have been out about four hours, and yet, he was not tired.

At first he thought it must be love—the inspiring presence of Little Owl—but she could not account for Uncle Jack's or the Rudd crew's energy. It must be Nukik, he thought. "Strength" Vincent Ologak had named the whale, no doubt for such a moment as this.

But the hours of paddling went on and on and weariness did set in. Roy slumped over his knees, Little Owl rested her paddle more often, and even Uncle Jack's back rounded. The Rudd crew did not lift their paddles as high as they had.

Musk Ox stood up.

"We are exhausted," he said. "We have a long way to go. Should we cut off from the whale and go for more help?"

"No!" Every voice.

"The waves are slopping into the boats," he went on. "We must save lives."

"We must save the Eskimo," Little Owl piped.

"Yes!" Every voice.

"Paddle!" called Lincoln.

"Paddle!" said Otis. The wind blew and gusted. The gulls departed. The seals did not surface. The walruses swam behind ice floes out of the wind. Lincoln, holding the oar in his now trembling hands, heard his friends grunt in pain as they slaved. But they would not give up.

"Left side, backwater. Right side, paddle." The umiaqs turned sharply and angled into the waves to make use of the power of the wind and current once more.

"How long have we been paddling?" Tigluk asked.

"Six hours," Kusiq answered. "And we're hours from home."

"The whale will soon spoil," Tigluk said to Lincoln. "In twenty-four hours it becomes too rotten to use."

"It's in ice water," Lincoln said. "It should stay fresh."

"Lotsa heat in that big body," Tigluk explained. "It can't escape through the insulating blubber and skin. It begins to boil and ferment in twelve hours.

"Paddle!"

The water splashed over Lincoln's knees and he angled closer into the wind. Suddenly, as if anugI, the wind, and sagvaq, the current, had at long last decided to co-operate, they got behind the boats and sped them along the ice edge. Camp could not be too far away.

"HO!" Uncle Jack was on his feet.

"Science perch!" He pointed to three small figures standing on a luminous cone of snow beyond a bench of sea ice.

"We're almost home, Lincoln," he called. "Your camp's around that point—and one of our hydrophones. I heard you driving tent spikes through the instrument—that's how I found you."

Barbara ran down from the perch and picked her way to the edge of the water to greet the whalers. She saw the gold beard of Jack James.

"Musk Ox!" she shouted. "What are you doing out there?"

"Get the mayor—the mayor of the North Slope—on the radio," he said, remembering Barrow had two mayors, one for the town, one for the entire borough. "Shout, 'Hallelujah! It's the Ologaks.' "

"Shout what?"

" 'Hallelujah! Ologak!' "

Barbara pulled off her face mask, stared across the choppy water and flipped on her hand radio.

"Mayor Kingik, this is science perch. Do you copy?"

"I copy you, science perch. Over."

"Hallelujah! Ologak!" she said.

"Tell her to send help," Lincoln said, but Barbara was climbing back to the perch.

"She has said all that is necessary," Little Owl said.

" 'Hallelujah! Ologak!' will bring all the help we need— the people of Barrow town. The ice will dance with people. We will have lots of help, lots of happy help."

"Paddle!" He could not kill a whale, but he could navigate. Maybe Little Owl could learn to love a navigator.

"Paddle, paddle." They were nearly home, and like all living things who are nearly home, the whalers got a new spurt of strength.

In an hour they made it into the cove with the help of anugI and sagvaq. Herds of seals swam to meet them. Lincoln took another look. They were not seals at all, but glorious, swiftly flying umiaqs. The other whale crews on the lead had heard the news and were coming to help. They were fresh and they were cheering. They drew up and roped to the tow rope.

All together the whaleboats made a glorious pageant as they moved across the purple sea as one great loving family. Lincoln had never seen anything so impressive in his life.

A two-way radio in the boat behind the Ologak umiaq crackled.

"Riley, do you copy me? Over."

"I copy you, Barbara. Over."

"Where are you? Over."

"I'm on the Beaufort Sea, bringing in a whale. What else should I do on my day off? Over."

"Riley, I am to read you this message," Barbara said. "Listen. Do you copy me?"

"Yes, I copy you, Barbara."

"Vincent Ologak has passed away. He died happy. He received the good news of Nukik, the whale of Barrow town. Over."

The Ologak crew sat in stunned silence.

"Riley, do you copy me? Over."

"Yes, Barbara. Yes."

"Can you announce the death of this great man out there on the water, wherever you are? Over."

"Roger. Over. Out." Slowly Chuck Riley lifted his arm and held up his hand.

"Naalaktuagitchi," he shouted, then in English, "Hear me!" His voice carried to several nearby boats. The crews stopped talking.

"Listen!"

"Listen! Listen!"

"Listen!"

That word was passed from boat to boat until there was no sound but the lap of waves and the call of gulls. Chuck Riley balanced on the harpooner's seat.

"Vincent Ologak is dead. Ologak crew, he knew of your great success. He died happy."

Riley's voice reached every ear, then rolled on out over the water and was lost in the frozen wilderness.

"Amen!" Otis Rudd belled out, and by ones, by threes, by eights, by twelves, the whalers rose and bowed their heads.

Lincoln squeezed his eyes shut. The ache inside him was so intense, he felt as if he were on fire.

"Take good care of Nukik, Vincent Ologak," he whispered into his ruff. "Take good care of Nukik." He leaned on the steering oar as the whalers lifted their paddles in tribute to the fallen leader. A low melodious sound arose, and for a moment Lincoln thought the whales were singing. But there were words—in English.

> *Mine eyes have seen the glory of the coming of the Lord;*
> *He is trampling out the vintage where the grapes of wrath*
>   *are stored;*
> *He hath loosed the fateful lightning of His terrible swift sword.*
>   *His truth is marching on.*
> *Glory, glory, Hallelujah!*
> *Glory, glory, Hallelujah!*
> *Glory, glory, Hallelujah!*
>   *His truth is marching on.*

TWELVE

Autaaq, the sharing

SNOW FELL quietly as the fleet of umiaqs towed the whale of Barrow town to the blue ice perch where Lincoln had stood six hours ago. It blurred the outlines of the boats and erased the difference between the ice and the sky. Where the sun shone through the snow clouds, circular rainbows appeared. In this gentle beauty the great whale came home to the people.

Lincoln climbed wearily out of the umiaq and tied it to a block of ice. He was a thousand years back in time, standing beside an armada of handmade whaling boats that bobbed on the sea. No machines or radios were visible, no telephone wires, no wooden houses. The sounds were ancient: people speaking Iñupiat, waves lapping, ice crackling. Lincoln put his head on his paddle and slept standing on his feet as he had seen Utik once do. Little Owl sat down and put her head on her knees. She too slept.

"Where's the block and tackle?" Musk Ox's voice.

"In this box." Little Owl was awake.

"Someone get the Ologak flags!" Tigluk.

Lincoln woke up. The few minutes of snatched sleep had refreshed him, and he glanced around to see what needed to be done. Uncle Jack and Little Owl were lifting a huge wooden block with its yards of tackle out of one of Weir's boxes, and Kusiq and Roy were hauling the umiaq to the sled. Lincoln hurried to help them. When they were done, Kusiq picked up the paddles, placed them in holes in the seats, and crossed them above the boat.

"We whale no more, the paddles say," Kusiq explained to Lincoln. "The Ologak crew has its gift from the sea."

Voices murmured in the distance, and over the top of the pressure ridge, down an ice valley, over the luminous blue ice, came the people of Barrow. To Lincoln they were works of art in their red, gold, blue and skin parkas, and in their boots, in their furs and mittens, as they flowed over the white seascape to honor their whale.

They moved in groups, and clusters, and one by one, to the edge of the lead. There they looked quietly down on their aġviQ.

"Two years," an elder said. "We have suffered for two years. The pain is over."

"Hallelujah! Hallelujah! Aarigaa—good all right! Hal-le-lu-u-jah!"

Musk Ox laid out the block and tackle and carried one end of the rope to the helpers at the whale. They tied the tackle around the tail stock. Musk Ox then picked up the other end, and was hauling it toward the ridge when an Eskimo who had celebrated with too much whiskey on the way from town walked up to him.

"No white man at the whale," he snarled. Jack turned to see who was speaking.

"Nukaaluk, brother," the man apologized, and put an arm around Musk Ox's shoulder. Lincoln was wondering what that was all about when Little Owl walked up.

"Did you get the Ologak flags?" Musk Ox asked her.

"Oh!" She put her mitten to her mouth. "I am manager. I forget." She ran into the tent and came out with two flags of emerald green on which two golden Xs were sewn.

"Annie's here!" Little Owl called gleefully to Musk Ox and Lincoln. "Oh, I give many thanks, Annie's here. She is boiling water for the ceremonial maktak the crew must eat here on the ice. She is making coffee for everyone— the whole town." She looked around with shining eyes. "There are all kinds of outsiders here—Mexicans, Blacks, Filipinos, Englishmen, even a scientist from the International Whaling Commission. That's nice." She fastened one of the flags on a pole and found Kusiq.

"You must raise the flag, brave harpooner," she said.

"Ask someone else," he answered. "I'm busy."

"Tradition," she reminded him. Kusiq smiled at her and picked up an ice chopper. He ran across the flats weaving in and out among the people, the flag fluttering and snapping. Climbing an ice block, he chipped a hole in its top for the flagpole, then asked someone to pass him up a bucket of slush. He poured it around the pole. The Eskimo cement froze in mere minutes and held the pole and flag firmly. Vincent Ologak was now here to be looked up to. But the flag hung limp. There was no wind, just snow. Without a billowing flag, Vincent Ologak's spirit was missing. Kusiq waved his hands, jumped up and down and blew—and as if summoned, anugI, the wind, gusted up the side of the ice hill. The flag unfurled and fluttered.

"Vincent Ologak!" Kusiq sang out.

"Vincent Ologak!" the people of Barrow cheered.

Kusiq ran down the ice, grabbed the shoulder of a boy about two years younger than he and spun him around.

"Orson," he said to his brother, "you are chosen to carry the flag to town and put it up on the top of Vincent's house." The boy's face was a mixture of confusion and joy.

"Me?" He grinned. "But you must do it."

"I am needed here," Kusiq said. "Time is running out for the whale. We must butcher it now. Take the orange snow machine."

"Did you really harpoon the aġviQ and kill it?" Orson asked. "Without a bomb?"

"He gave himself."

"How did you do it? Show me."

"Get going." Kusiq grinned modestly. "It was nothing." But he knew better, and so did everyone else. He heard his name on many lips. Many people were pointing him out.

"He used an ancient lance," a man said. "Good lancer, that Kusiq all right."

"No gun. No bomb," someone else added. Kusiq concentrated on Orson, pretending not to hear, but he was bursting with pride. He was a harpooner, a whaler, a provider of life for his people.

"Get going, Orson," Kusiq said again, and gently put his hand under his brother's chin to close the mouth that had dropped wide open. "We start a new tradition, young brother."

"A new tradition?" Little Owl said. "I heard you. None of that," she chided. "We want no new traditions. We can't keep up with the old ones." Kusiq laughed and, picking her up in his arms, hugged her to him. The red in her cheeks brightened.

Lincoln Noah Stonewright saw the warm embrace, turned away and watched the flag flap in the wind. A door was closing in his face. His mentor was dead, the whale was taken, the people of Barrow were whole again. They were laughing and busy with plans for feasting and dancing. He was not needed. The myth of Nukik coming to him had died with the elder—and Little Owl had a hero in the best of her tradition. He, Lincoln, was just a tanik in a parka on the ice.

He began to feel uneasy. He had not realized how much his peace of mind and safety had depended upon Vincent Ologak. The elder had seen to it that he was accepted by the crew. He had seen to it that a myth surrounded him. He had seen to it that he learned what to do in whale camp. Now Lincoln was alone and un-protected among people who really did not like outsiders.

"How do people survive bigotry?" he asked himself.

Then he saw Uncle Jack. He was here. He was ac-cepted. How had he managed? He walked over to him as Otis Rudd joined him.

"The ice is thin here," Otis said to Jack. "That's a fifty-ton whale."

"Dangerous," Jack answered. "But we don't have time to find a better landing spot. The whale will soon begin to rot. Got any suggestions?"

"The ice is thicker near the ridge. We could pull the whale up against it. I have done that before. It works all right . . . if there is any predicting the ice."

"Good idea," said Jack.

"So that's how you do it," Lincoln said to his uncle.

"Do what?"

"Be accepted by the Eskimo. You learn from them."

"Everything I know about the Arctic I have learned from these scientists of the north. But the most important thing I have learned from them is sharing—not only food, but knowledge—and love. We need each other's warmth and wisdom." He put his arm around Lincoln's shoulder and said, "See that group of men over there by the ridge? They need you." Lincoln grinned as he joined them. Uncle Jack was still a tanik: He had told him what to do.

The men had hauled one of the pulleys to the foot of the ridge. Nearby were men chipping the ice, and several were admiring Weir's block and tackle.

"This one is old all right," said a gray-headed whaler. "It is good."

"It's from the Yankee whaling days," another man said. "Weir told me that."

"We learned a lot from those Yankee whalers," an elder commented. "My great-grandfather and his crew had to butcher some whales in the sea. They couldn't pull the big ones like this aġviQ out of the water until the Yankees showed them how to use a block and tackle."

Lincoln picked up an ice chopper and joined the men who were chipping. It turned out that they were making a U-shaped tunnel. This would be the brace for the block and tackle.

"That bit of ingenuity in using the ice for a brace," Lincoln thought, "came from the Eskimos, I'll bet." He grinned and chipped carefully.

He was working with a handsome Eskimo in his thirties. Without discussing it they were taking turns at the job. First Lincoln chipped, then the man, nodding to each other as they shared the work and the good feeling abroad in this awesome pageant of cooperation.

"Are you through to the other side yet, Mayor?" someone asked Lincoln's partner.

"Almost," Mayor Elijah Kingik said, then got down on his belly and chopped on.

An hour ago Elijah Kingik had been sitting in his office in Borough Hall talking on the telephone with Juneau, the state capital, when Barbara radioed, "Hallelujah! Ologak!" He had flipped on the CB and told the Eskimo

CB fans and the radio station that the Ologaks had taken a whale. Then he had called Annie and learned that Weir was with her. He asked if they wanted to ride out with him. They did. He took off his three-piece suit and put on his whaling clothes. The last thing he did before leaving was to turn off his computer. Now he was on his belly, chopping.

"Got it," he called. "We're through!"

Two men hauled the larger of two wheels to the tunnel and roped it. The other wheel was near the whale. The pull would be the people, the whale the resistance. The pulleys on the block and tackle would divide the tonnage by five, making the weight to be pulled a manageable ten tons for the hundreds of people, instead of an impossible fifty.

When the ropes to the block and tackle were secured,

the whale was ready to come up on the ice. Almost instantly the men, women and young people leaped down from their perches and ice piles and picked up the hauling rope. Little Owl beckoned to Lincoln, and he grabbed hold.

"Walk away!" a senior whaler called. The people pulled; and slowly, slowly the sea gift came out of the water and up onto the ice. Mayor Kingik pulled and waved on the people of Barrow town.

"All hands!" The villagers gave a last effort, and the whale moved on. The snow thickened. The people tugged. The gift was not freely given, but at last it lay at the base of the ridge.

"HO!" Kusiq shouted. "Whale landed! AġviQtut!"

"Hallelujah! Hallelujah!"

The ropes were dropped, and the Eskimos circled their whale. Swept along with them were Lincoln and Little Owl.

"I'm sad," Lincoln said. Little Owl took his hand.

"You mustn't be. See how happy I am? Feel the celebration and ceremony all around you? Thank you, Lincoln Noah Stonewright. A whale did come to you."

A friend grabbed Little Owl's other hand and pulled her off into the crowd. Lincoln walked over to the whale.

A little girl ran away from her mother and stood on tiptoes to touch the great mouth of the bowhead.

"I can't see the whale," she protested. "It's too big." Lincoln agreed with her. The whale loomed upward twelve feet. It stretched fifty feet from lower jaw to tail, and like the little girl, Lincoln could not take in the whole creature. It was better that way.

Kusiq went to the head of the whale and lifted his whale knife, a square steel blade on a twelve-foot pole. Other whale knives rose like ceremonial torchlights above the whale of Barrow town. They were held by a very select group, those who still knew how to divide the gift.

Tigluk, Roy, Little Owl and Musk Ox joined Kusiq at the head of the whale, and the people of Barrow stopped talking.

Slowly Kusiq lifted his hand and poured a cup of water into the mouth of the aġviQ. An old man came forward, his head bare.

"Praise the sea," he said, softly praying. "Praise the sun, and the wind, and the current. Praise the air and all things that give us life. Forgive us, great whale. Amen."

Quickly Kusiq climbed to the top of the whale and cut a wedge of maktak from the center back. He took a bite, sliced it and passed pieces to Tigluk, Roy, Little Owl and Musk Ox, the successful crew.

"Where's Lincoln?" Tigluk asked. People pointed him out.

Tigluk beckoned him, and Lincoln made his way to the head of the whale.

"My friend," Tigluk said, jumping down to meet him. He opened his arms and enveloped him. All anger had vanished from Tigluk, and Lincoln was surprised to note that his own resentment for the things Tigluk had done was also gone. Kusiq leaned down, gave them each a hand, and pulled them up.

"Eat this and celebrate the whale," he said, putting a piece of maktak between Lincoln's lips. "The whale came to you, Lincoln Noah Stonewright. He came to the great-great-grandson of Nora Ologak Stonewright." The maktak was black and pink. Lincoln chewed it thoughtfully. The people of Barrow watched him in silence.

"It's delicious," he finally said. "Like melted fish and butter." The whalers laughed, and the people clapped for the very sensible tanik.

"Good boy all right," an elder said.

"Now, to work," said Kusiq, picking up his whale knife. "We have very little time."

The whaling butchers climbed up on the aġviQ with their twelve-foot-long knives and, with the skill of surgeons, carved according to the fifteen-hundred-year-old tradition. Lincoln watched in fascination, then went off to find Uncle Jack.

"For the Nalukataq celebration!" Kusiq announced as the area around the blowhole and the slice behind the eye were severed and dropped onto the ice. Jack saw Lincoln approaching and handed him a heavy iron meat hook like his own. Jack snagged his into the huge piece of blubber and pulled. Lincoln snagged his in and pulled. It would not budge. Four other men got their hooks into the maktak and all pulled. It moved. They ran, going faster and faster, pulling the gift through the valley the villagers had carved in the pressure ridge so the whale could be pulled out to the flat. There, almost a hundred snow machines and sleds were parked in a half circle. This was the dividing arena, and the people were waiting respectfully for their share of the gift. One of Annie's adopted daughters showed Lincoln and Jack where to put their chunk of maktak; then they turned and ran back to the whale.

"For all the crews who are whaling," Kusiq announced as each of many slabs were cut and dropped. The butchers went to the head.

"For the captain, the tender parts below the mouth," Kusiq said, then thought a moment. "Take it to Bertha.

"For the harpooner, a flipper.

"For the Ologak crew, the other flipper.

"For the Christmas feast."

While the whale was being divided, Annie and several more of her adopted daughters passed out cooked maktak to the crews and steaming hot coffee, sugar and cream to everyone else.

"For the owner and operator of the block and tackle," Kusiq called. Weir came forward and hooked his own gift. When Little Owl saw him, she ran joyfully to help.

"For the crews to take back to your tent sites and eat on the ice." The butchers worked on.

"For the celebration at Annie Ologak's home tonight."

Lincoln could not believe how swiftly the enormous animal was divided. He and the other men and women with hooks were running the huge slabs of maktak to the dividing arena every minute or so. When the maktak was gone, the meat was cut up and hauled off in the same manner.

Within four hours nothing remained but ribs, skull and baleen.

"Half of the baleen to the successful captain," Kusiq announced, "half to the crew members who helped pull the aġviQ home. Lots of you."

Mayor Kingik walked up to Musk Ox.

"The ice is breaking near the tail of the whale. It's time to go."

Jack handed his hook to the high-school principal who was standing by and went with the mayor to examine the crack.

"Lots of taniks," Jack said, as he greeted many of his lower-forty-eight friends: schoolteachers, nurses and doctors from the hospital, the radio disc jockey, other scientists, as well as the Mexicans who waited on tables in the Mexican restaurant and Filipinos who worked on construction jobs.

"This United Nations assembly is Vincent Ologak's last request," the mayor said. "He told Bertha to invite all the outsiders to the landing of the whale of Barrow town. 'At the whale,' he said, 'will we understand each other.' That's what he said."

"How right he is," said Jack.

They stopped before a wide chasm in the ice under what remained of the tail. The crack was extensive. It circled the cove.

"How long do we have?" Jack asked.

"Another hour . . . maybe."

THIRTEEN

The spirit of the whale of Barrow

LITTLE OWL pushed back her hood to watch the baleen as it was carried triumphantly across the sagging ice to Captain Vincent Ologak's sled. The long graceful filters pranced and tossed like ponies. They meant timeless pleasure to Little Owl: baskets she would weave with Annie, legends to be carved on the springy blue-black blades and jewelry to be fashioned from the glistening black stalks with their ivory-white bases. The artwork would be beautiful. This baleen was extraordinarily rich in color and shine.

The snow had almost stopped falling, the sky had brightened and the eider ducks and gulls who had been sleeping on the ice awoke and called to each other. The guillemots stretched their legs and wings, preparing to fly on. There are not many different kinds of birds in the Arctic, but there are many of each kind. Billions freckle the sea ice in spring. Not far from the birds the seals yawned. It was wake-up time, not by light signals but by internal clocks. The wild things had had enough sleep. They would fly or swim on, eating and napping when they needed to. At noon and midnight they would take longer sleeps.

When the maktak and whale meat had been divided, only the ribs and the skull remained. Every other part and piece had an owner; even the heart, the liver and the stomach. The whalers would share their portions of the whale with relatives and friends, who would in turn share it with their relatives and friends, and many Eskimos would share with the taniks. Some owners would freeze their portions in their ice cellars, rooms dug deep in the frozen Arctic soil that remains at eighteen degrees Fahrenheit the year around. Others would store their gift in their electric freezers.

As the birds woke up, the women began to gather around the arches of ribs that stood dark red and majestic against the white snow. The gleaning time was at hand. Kusiq, the harpooner, had raised his whale knife. When he dropped it, the women and anyone else, tanik or Eskimo, could rush in and carve off the last scraps of meat. Little Owl did not like this part of the ceremony. She found it demeaning to the whale. The people fought like gulls over the tidbits. The civilized system of distribution that had been worked out so carefully over the centuries broke down at gleaning time, and fights erupted.

But she was not the one to change tradition. She sighed over what was to come and watched Kusiq. He held his long knife high as he watched the last pieces of baleen bob down the blue-and-dawn-pink ice valley to safety. Forty people carried the six hundred filters, which were anywhere from five to ten feet long. The last ones formed an arch of triumph on the ice.

"I see the spirit of the aġviQ going through that arch as he returns to the sea," Little Owl said aloud to no one. But Lincoln was listening.

"So do I," he said. "Wow, butchering pigs at the Dutchess County Fair was never like this."

"What is the Dutchess County Fair?"

"When you come to Harvard, I'll take you to it . . . but you'll be disappointed."

"Lincoln," Little Owl said as she waited for the gleaning. "Did you ever find out why Musk Ox disappeared into Barrow?"

"Sort of," he said, startled by her question. Then, with a chuckle, he realized that the people of the ice knew a great deal about him.

"I think," he said, glad to discuss the mystery, "that he changed his mind about Eskimo whaling. He was embarrassed to tell me."

"That's hardly a reason," Little Owl said, putting on her dark glasses as the sun brightened and burned off the last threads of the snow cloud.

"Well, how about this?" Lincoln decided to test another theory he had evolved. "Bertha told me that Musk Ox and Vincent Ologak had a terrible argument. That might have upset him. It would me."

"Not that. It was a good argument. Vincent convinced

Musk Ox that the Eskimo must whale for our culture to survive. He told him there were now enough bowheads for the Eskimo to harvest a few. He said the Eskimo would never kill off the great whale as the white man had done. The Eskimo would not push it to extinction. After that, Musk Ox joined the science research team."

"Well, then, why?" Lincoln asked. "He just came up here and vanished as far as my family is concerned." He rubbed his chin. "Do you know why?"

"He got married."

"Oh!" Lincoln thought a moment. "What's that got to do with anything? He could have told me that. I'd understand that!"

Little Owl pushed her sunglasses up on her forehead and looked at him with surprise. "He thought you knew."

"How could I know if he didn't write and tell me?"

"He told your mother, Annie said."

"He did? She never told me."

Lincoln stood somberly as he let this sink in.

"Why wouldn't she tell me?"

Little Owl shuffled her feet and replaced her glasses. "Possibly," she said, "because he married an Eskimo, my cousin Lottie."

Lincoln felt as if he had been hit by a snowball. Images tumbled around in his head. He saw great-great-grandmother Nora, the Arctic, the paintings on the walls of his home. He saw Tigluk and the empty bullet chamber of his own gun. He saw Roy's hands around his throat, he saw the anger in the drunk man's eyes when he spotted

Uncle Jack's blond beard and the change on his face when he saw that he was his "brother" in spirit, married as he was to an Eskimo. His thoughts kept turning, and up came his mother's face. She had a piece of tape over her mouth. She could not talk to Lincoln. She could not tell him that Nora was an Iñupiat or that his beloved Uncle Jack had married an Eskimo. And apparently his father had not wanted to upset her, so he had not told him either. Lincoln felt very sorry for them.

"My family needs a whale," he said softly. "They *really* do."

Kusiq lowered his whaling knife. The women ran, elbowing their way to the enormous ribs. They cut and slashed with their ulus and filled plastic bags with the good meat. A few stole full bags when the gleaners were not looking.

"I thought all fighting stopped when a whale was taken," Lincoln said as he watched the scene. "This is a mess."

"This is ancient," Little Owl said glumly. "We are back to the beginning, before the earth turned over and the wolves were the people." Then she brightened.

"But this passes, just as the darkness did when the world turned over. Tonight you will find love and friendship at the feast at Annie Ologak's house—although the family mourns." She knocked the snow off her ruff. "Even your mother would be welcome." They smiled at each other, but not without pain.

Tigluk and Roy had taken off their parkas during the hot work of butchering. They were now talking together earnestly in their T-shirts, even though the temperature was only a few degrees above zero. Presently they came to some agreement and searched the faces of the crowd, spotted Little Owl and Lincoln and, smiling broadly, joined them.

"What's up?" Lincoln asked.

"We have something for you, Lincoln Noah," Tigluk said. He took from his pocket a smooth piece of ivory as big as his fist. It was creamy white, shaped like a gently curved hand and very shiny. He put it in Lincoln's hand.

"This is for you," he said.

"What is it?" Lincoln asked. "It's really beautiful."

"A bone that lies in the ear of the whale. It balances him and helps him hear the sounds in the sea."

"And," added Roy, "it brings the vibrations from the people to him. He knows to whom to give himself."

Lincoln gently turned the rare object over.

"This instrument heard you," Tigluk said. "We thought you ought to have it."

"Thank you." He was unable to say more.

"Off the ice!" Mayor Kingik called.

The women stopped gleaning and looked in fright at the mayor, who had more or less taken over the captain's role. His words were to be taken seriously. They rounded up their children, stuffed their plastic bags of precious meat into their gunny sacks, grabbed the big rib bones and hurried toward the grounded ice.

The Ologak kitchen was hauled to a sled. The tent went down and was packed on top of the kitchen. There was no time to load the skins. Everyone was running to get off the booming, moving ice that was sagging under the weight of the last great bone, the skull.

Musk Ox caught up with the mayor, and together they escorted dawdling gleaners and children through the ice pass to the dividing arena. Little Owl reached the valley and stopped.

"What's the matter?" Lincoln asked her.

"We can't leave yet." She glanced at the mayor. He was herding two little children, his back to her.

"Lincoln Noah," she said, "the spirit of the whale has not been set free." She turned and ran toward the whale. Lincoln followed her.

"Off the ice!" Mayor Kingik happened to turn around and see Little Owl and Lincoln running to the whale. "Chuck Riley," he shouted.

"Sir?" came a reply from nearby.

"Get Tom Albert on your radio. Tell him to get out here on the double."

"Little Owl," Lincoln yelled as they ran, "come back. The ice is going out." He ran faster, reached for her parka, missed and found himself in two inches of slush beside the great skull of the aġviQ. It stood eight feet high and was twenty feet long—the bowhead is almost half head—a magnificent sight alone on the ice that seemed to hold it dear and claim it.

The mayor and Musk Ox untied the umiaq and ran with it to the water.

Little Owl threw her weight against the skull. It did not budge.

"Help me, Lincoln. We must push this sauniQ into the sea."

Lincoln did not stop to think. Little Owl needed him. He ran back a dozen steps, sprinted and threw his weight against the great bone. The ice tipped and slowly slid the skull toward the water.

"I bless the great spirit of Nukik," Little Owl said. "Return to your people, aġviQ. Enter into them and become a new whale. Amen. Good-bye."

The bone slid faster and faster. The ice tilted more steeply and dumped all three into the sea.

The raucous blattering of a helicopter sounded over-head as Lincoln scrambled up onto the ice floe where the whale had once lain. His boots and mittens had filled with water, but his body was still dry inside his mass of clothing.

"Little Owl!"

"Here." He turned around. She was stretched out on her belly on the whale floe, looking up at him with an apologetic smile on her face. He pulled her into the center of the tippy floe, and they sat, feet out straight, looking at each other.

And there in the sky was a helicopter—on the water an umiaq. Lincoln waved to the sky bird as the chill began to reach him. Little Owl cried, "Ataata," and broke into tears. Weir was alone kneeling in the center of the boat, paddling calmly toward her. This was his sea, her sea—all was well.

The wind from the helicopter blades whipped up the water and beat against Lincoln's already cold face, making it colder. The mechanical bird hovered and slowly descended. A rope ladder was pushed out the open door. It fell almost into Lincoln's hands. He grabbed it and held it steady for Little Owl.

"Take hold!" he yelled over the copter roar. "The new isn't all bad." Little Owl shook her head.

"Come with me, Lincoln," she said as Weir silently placed the umiaq beside the floe. "Come back to your people with me." She tugged his wet, freezing snow shirt.

"No, Little Owl. No. That's crazy. Don't go in the umiaq. The copter's warm. It's good. It has everything you need—dry clothing, food, medicine." Instantly he saw that his words were not the right ones. They brought pain to Little Owl's face. She pulled away from him.

"Nagliksaagnaqtuaq. Aitchuutikssraitkapta,"* Little Owl said. She steadied herself on Weir's extended paddle and stepped into the umiaq.

"Little Owl, please, please. Speak English, please. Why are you closing me out?"

"Lincoln!" the loudspeaker blasted. "Tom Albert here; Chief of the Sea Rescue Squad. Get yourself up that ladder!"

"Little Owl, come with me!" Lincoln called.

"Get yourself up here!" roared Tom Albert.

Little Owl pulled a fur over her. Lincoln stepped on the rope ladder and climbed halfway; then some mech-

[205]

anism took hold and he was pulled swinging and twisting into the warm body of the helicopter.

A rescue volunteer pulled off Lincoln's ice-crusted boots, pants and parka and threw a blanket around him as he leaned over the observation bubble and looked down on Weir and Little Owl. They were all alone on the Arctic Ocean, the last Eskimos on earth going their way in harmony with their world.

"Mayor Kingik, this is Tom Albert. Do you copy?"

"I copy you, Albert. Over."

"We have effected a rescue. We have Lincoln.

"Weir Amaogak has effected a rescue too. He has Little Owl. Both kids are in good shape. Over."

"Hallelujah!" said Mayor Kingik. "Come on home. There's lotsa maktak. Over."

That sunny night Lincoln searched for Little Owl in the happy, singing crowd that had gathered around Annie Ologak's house. He had to know why she had closed him out. Was it revealed in her Iñupiat words? He thought so. She was not at the stove with Annie or even outside with the kids who were doing the one-foot-high kick. Tigluk said she had suffered no ill effects from her dunking because Weir had had his survival gear with him. Tigluk thought she was with Bertha and Vincent Ologak's children and grandchildren joining them in their grief. She was not at their house, although she had been there, according to Mayor Kingik. Utik said he had just recently seen her dancing with Kusiq outside the Community Center. Lincoln hurried off to find her and make amends.

As he was leaping around and over the mud puddles of the swift spring melt, Uncle Jack intercepted him.

"Lincoln Noah," he said, "I've been looking for you. Come on home with me and meet your lovely Aunt Lottie, my wife."

Lincoln glanced toward the Community Center, then turned somewhat reluctantly and caught stride with Uncle Jack. After all, this was what he had come to Barrow to do.

In the bright light of four A.M., when the feasting was done, when the drums had stopped beating and the dancers' feet were still, when Lincoln and Uncle Jack had righted their misunderstanding and Lincoln had met and laughed with Aunt Lottie, he crawled into a bed in Uncle Jack's apartment and took the ivory bone from his pocket.

He rubbed it. It was real. He could see it and feel it. But it was also unreal: as unreal as Little Owl going off in the umiaq when the helicopter had offered so much, as unreal as his not finding her again, as the whale that had come to him, as the ice he had fought and the wind and sun and current he had dwelled with. Here in this modern apartment so much like those at home, he knew he would never understand the beautiful people of the ice. But why? he asked himself, why?

He sat straight up in bed, knowing at last what Little Owl had said to him as she made her choice. He had heard it every day in the silent language of the whalers. And it put a darkness between them.

*"It is a real hardship when we have nothing to give."

Iñupiat Pronouncing
Vocabulary and Glossary

Iñupiat Pronouncing Vocabulary and Glossary

aarigaa (ah ŕig ah)—that's good

aġviQ (aŕg vik)—bowhead whale

AġviQ qaitchuq (aŕg vik kí chuk)—The whale gave itself.

aġviqtut (ahg vík toot)—The whale is landed.

aitchunsiaq (ite choon sée ak)—the sea gift

aiviQ (éye vik)—walrus

anugI (ahn oó gee)—the wind

aquun (ah cóon)—the rudder

Ataata (ah tá ta)—Grandfather

autaaq (ów tok)—the sharing

aullaaġviQ (owl láug vik)—whaling camp

iglu (íg loo)—house

Inianniik (in eé an neek)—the hills southeast of Barrow

Iñupiat (in yóu pea it)—Eskimo people and language

Ivuqpagman ivuvlugu inuillu payagniu-lammata (ee vuke payg man ee voov loo goo ee noo eel loo pay yag new-lawm may tay)—When a lot of pressure ridges formed, the ice piled up.

Karuk (káy rook)—hit-on-the-head

Kingik (kíng ik)

Kusiq (koós ik)

maktak (muk tuk)—blubber

naalaktuagitchi (nah lake taw geet chee)—listen; pay attention

Nagliksaagnaqtuaq. Aitchuutikssraitkapta. (nog lik sok nak too ock. ite choo tiks srite kap tay.)—It is a real hardship when we have nothing to give.

Nalukataq (nal oo ka ták)—whale festival

natchiagruk (nate chi a grook)—infant seal

natchiQ (nát chik)—ringed seal

nauligaun (now lee gówn)—whale harpoon

nigliviK (neég li vik)—white-fronted goose

niqislauraq (nik is laúw rake)—a lot of food

nukaaluk (noo ká luke)—younger brother

Nukik (nóo kik)—"strength"

nutagaq (noot ay gák)—the young whalers

Ologak (olé e gak)

paniqtaq (pán ik take)—dried meat or fish

piayaaq aġviQ (pie ya aḱk aḱg vik)—young whale

piqaluyk (pea chá loo ik)—old, saltless ice

puktaaq (pook tá ik)—iceberg

qanitchaq (koon ni chúk)—a small windowless room that serves as the entrance to a house

qasuaq pilik (kée sack píll ik)—bad calm

Sagniq (ság nik)

sagvaq (ság vuk)—current

sauniQ (sow nik)—skull

siku (seé koo)—pack ice

Siku anayanaqtuq! (seé koo ana ýan ak took)—Get off the ice!

Silam, nature-m. (síl am nah too rem)—It is natural.

stuaqpak (stuak pák)—supermarket

tanik (tún ik)—white person

Tigluk (tíg look)

ugruk (oóg rook)—bearded seal

Ukpik (ook pik)—"snowy owl"

ulu (oo loo)—woman's multipurpose semicircular knife

umialik (oóm ee aḱ lik)—whaling captain

umiaq (oóm me ak)—skin boat

Utik (oó tik)

Weir Amaogak (weir ah má oh guk)